MASKED IN MYSTERY

REVEALING THE TRUTH

SRIPRIYA MADIRAJU

Made with ♥ on the Notion Press Platform
www.notionpress.com

Contents

Contents

Foreword

As I sit down to write this foreword for my daughter's debut novel, I am filled with pride and admiration. I vividly recall the time when Sripriya embarked on this journey in ninth grade and completed the novel around the beginning of tenth grade. Despite the demands of school and extracurricular activities, she poured her heart and soul into crafting this tale. As a parent, witnessing her dedication and determination has been truly inspiring.

What strikes me most about "Masked in Mystery" is that it is entirely the product of Sripriya's imagination and hard work - from the initial concept to the final draft. She insisted on keeping the editing process within the family, trusting me to provide feedback and guidance. It's a privilege I deeply cherish.

Although I aimed for its release almost 18 months ago, my own commitments kept me occupied, and it took longer than anticipated for this book to finally take shape.

Now that Sripriya is older, her perspective may have evolved. However, as parents, we believe in honoring her original version. Hence, this novel represents a snapshot of her creativity and talent during her early high school years, capturing the essence of her thoughts at that time.

As I delved into the story, I found myself captivated by the twists and turns that unfolded with each page. What really amazed me was the depth of my child's curiosity, creativity, and logical thinking.

To my dear daughter, I extend my heartfelt congratulations on the publication of your first novel. I have no doubt that this marks just the beginning of your literary journey. May "Masked in

Mystery" find its way into the hearts of readers everywhere, just as it has found its way into mine.

Rekha Madiraju
9th April 2024

CHAPTER 1
Lights everywhere I go

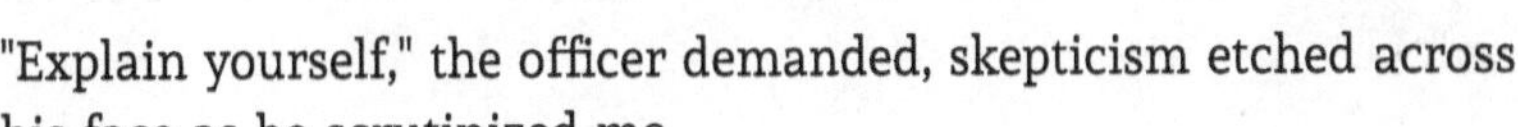

"Explain yourself," the officer demanded, skepticism etched across his face as he scrutinized me.

Panic surged within me as I had been through this interrogation before.

"I've told you repeatedly, I just arrived in New York. Look at my tickets. I am not a thief!" I pleaded desperately.

Reluctantly, the NYPD officer examined my proof, his stern facade giving way to a begrudging acceptance.

"Alright, you can go," he grumbled. "You do bear a striking resemblance to the suspect. She's a young, blonde college student with curly hair, a slim build, and decent height."

Eager to prove my innocence and perhaps fulfill a secret dream, I offered my assistance.

"Is there any way I can help with the investigation?" I asked, employing my most convincing puppy dog eyes, but the officer rebuffed my offer.

"No way, kid. You can leave now," he dismissed.

Then, in a moment of realization, I exclaimed, "There she is!"

My finger pointed to a young and pretty woman making a swift escape from Grand Central Terminal. The officer swiftly apprehended her, her guilt now undeniable.

It was a stark reminder that appearances could indeed be deceptive.

Myriad thoughts rushed through my head as I watched the arrest unfold.

Why would she steal? She was beautiful, and I imagined everyone wanted to befriend her.

The officer returned to the cab station where I was waiting, and I snapped back to reality, only to be met with a bewildered stare.

Politely, he offered me a ride, but the thought of going home to my stepmother in a police vehicle did not appeal to me.

"No thank you, Officer," I declined, slipping into my cab.

During my vacations, Mom spared me the discomfort of traveling to New York by coming to visit me in California.

This was my first time in New York, and the traffic jam that accompanied it gave me a headache. I found myself yearning to meet my stepmother at that very moment.

Finally, I reached home to find my stepmother, her arms crossed and a disapproving glare fixed upon me. The irony was not lost on me.

"Mom, I can explain. There was this NYPD officer," I began, but she interrupted, saying, "What took you so long? You should have been home by nine!"

I recounted the entire story to her, from the police officer's scrutiny to the arrest of the criminal. She gave me a warm, loving hug. It was then that I realized how much I had missed her.

"So, how is New York treating you, Mom?" I inquired.

"It's different," she replied. " Three years have been ample time for me to develop a deep affection for the city. I'm enjoying my work here. It is always bustling and lively. I never feel lonely, especially since I am part of the Community Welfare group for Green Avenue, our neighborhood. I have missed my little Shelly," she added with a smile.

I gave her a peck on the cheek and entered our apartment.

"Wow! This apartment is so cool. The design is contemporary, but the sofa is..." I began, but Mom cut in casually with, "Yup! Apartments are pretty much the same here. How's California? Are you enjoying college?"

I spoke of my love for California and the friends I had made at UC Davis.

"Mom, do you want to play a board game with me?" I asked.

She yawned, tired from her day.

"Sorry, darling, but I can hardly keep my eyes open. We will play in the morning for sure. Good night!"

"Good night, Mom! I will read a book. And I will wake up a little late tomorrow," I informed her.

Settling onto the plush sofa, I retrieved the mystery novel I had been reading. How thrilling it would be to be a part of a mystery like the one I had witnessed earlier. My mind raced with possibilities for the ending.

Eventually, I tore myself away from the book, got up, and walked to the window. The cool breeze brushed against my face, and I savored the fresh air. The vibrant lights of New York spread out before me, a mesmerizing spectacle. Though it was 1AM, it felt like 7PM. Indeed, New York was the city that never slept, a place where the crime rate was high yet the people remained jovial and exuberant. It promised to be a captivating summer vacation.

With that thought, I resumed reading the novel but inevitably succumbed to sleep.

CHAPTER 2
A not so well-planned tour

To be honest, I never expected my mom to disrupt my peaceful sleep at the crack of dawn, especially during my vacation!

"Shelly Peterson, get off the sofa! It is 6, and you are still in bed. Don't you want to play that board game?" my mom shouted. I had dozed off on the couch without realizing it.

"Mom, it's only 6AM! I arrived just yesterday and did not get enough sleep," I protested. Mom, being Mom, was determined to get me out of bed. She not-so-gently removed my blanket and practically yanked me off the sofa. I grumbled as I reluctantly woke up on the wrong side of the bed.

"Why on earth did you wake up your exhausted daughter so early when she explicitly said she'd relax the next day?" I complained.

"I must not have heard that," Mom replied with a mischievous grin. "Anyway, I woke you up because I want to give you a tour of the magnificent New York City!"

"The 'magnificent' New York?" I retorted sarcastically. I quickly got dressed when I caught a whiff of Mom's specialty pancakes. "Mom, I have to admit, what I missed more than anything else is your pancakes," I said with a smile.

"Oh, come on!" Mom said, playfully nudging me. We both shared a hearty laugh. I devoured the first serving within seconds, leaving Mom staring at me in amazement.

As I enjoyed my meal, Mom hit me with the second surprise of the day, or rather, a "shock." "Well, honey, I don't think I can give you a tour now. I have a sudden committee meeting."

"MOM!" I growled. Just then, the doorbell rang. I wondered who could be visiting our house at 6:45 in the morning.

"Go answer it, dear," Mom said. I protested, but her stern look left me with no choice. I grudgingly went to the door and was surprised to find my two childhood best friends waiting outside. I was dumbfounded. "Was this a dream?" I pinched my cheek to confirm it was not. And I regretted doing so.

"It's not a dream, silly," Kyle and Natasha said in unison. I hugged them tightly and did not let go of them. "OMG! What are you guys doing here?" I squealed.

"I moved to New York a month ago," Kyle explained. "I informed Mrs. Peterson about my plan, and she instructed me not to tell you."

Mom gave a cheeky wink and got back to cooking more pancakes.

"That's why Mom woke me up at 6! What about you, Nats? Did you move here too?" I asked Natasha.

"No, my dad lives in New York, and my mom is in Jersey. They got divorced few years back, so I must keep shuffling between the two. Summers in New York and Christmases in Jersey," Natasha replied with a sigh. I hated seeing my best friends sad.

"I'm so sorry, Nats. If I had known, I would have tried to keep your mind off it," I said.

"Shelly, I've come to terms with it. Do not worry. We have a lot of catching up to do!" Natasha said with joy.

"Wait a minute, kiddos, have breakfast. I have made some pancakes," Mom said.

"Pancakes! I remember Mrs. Peterson's pancakes. They are the best in the world, to die for!" Kyle exclaimed, immediately digging into them.

Natasha admired the pancakes and said, "Seriously, Mrs. Peterson, why did you make such delish pancakes? They look so... I'm on a diet."

"Do they not look scrumptious or delicious, Natasha?" Mom asked innocently, not understanding the term 'delish.' I explained it to her, and then Mom thanked Nats.

"Nats, you're already so slim! Do you really need to diet? Eat up, or you will regret it later!" Kyle chimed in, halfway through his meal.

"Ugh, fine! If I gain weight, it is on you, Shelly," Natasha said. I tried to clarify that it was Kyle who... but was disrupted by the sounds of their enthusiastic eating.

After our meal, we reminisced about our school days, expressing our longing for each other despite forming new friendships.

"Anyway, was the New York tour just a ruse? If it was, I'm going to take a short nap," I said.

"Wait!" Kyle cried. "That wasn't a lie. We have an itinerary planned!"

"Pass," I replied, attempting to escape. Natasha grasped my wrist, pulling me back. "Who wouldn't want a tour of New York?" she asked.

"Not me! I've seen it all last night. New York doesn't deserve a second chance. The traffic, the crime, and I was almost blamed for..." I began before Kyle intercepted with excitement.

"New York has so much more to offer, Shelly. I'm sure you'll love it soon," he reassured me.

"I'm not so sure. I love California, and you should come visit. I've settled there, and drumroll!" I said, prompting Kyle to oblige. "I have a job!"

Mom was taken aback and said, "What—"

"No—" Natasha began.

"Way!" Kyle shouted. Their synchronized responses never failed to amuse.

"Which company?" Mom asked, breaking the silence.

"I have a job at Apple, though it's not in software. I'm in marketing," I clarified.

"But it's Apple! I am so proud of you, Shell!" Natasha exclaimed, enveloping me in a tight hug. "Little Shelly's all grown up!" teased Kyle.

"Oh, please! I'm older than you," I retorted.

"I'm jealous," Kyle admitted.

"Will you help us out too?" Natasha asked, flashing an adorable puppy-dog face.

"Of course! If you let me take a nap," I agreed.

"Whatever, sister," Natasha replied. With Kyle's help, she pulled me out for the second time that day, and I was less than thrilled.

"Don't wander off, kiddos. New York is like a maze. Once you are lost, there is no way out," Mom warned.

"We got this, Mrs. Peterson and we aren't kids anymore," Kyle assured her.

"Shelly, you do know the way home, right?" Mom asked.

"Yes, absolutely," I affirmed, though I was slightly uncertain. This was my first visit to Mom's place in New York.

"I'm responsible for all three of you, you know that, right?" Mom pointed at our faces as if we were criminals.

"Yes, ma'am," Kyle and Natasha replied, and we headed out without listening to Mom's further warnings. I didn't look back because I didn't want to see how Mom would react.

"Why was Mom saying she's responsible for both of you?" I inquired.

"Oh, didn't you know?" Kyle asked.

"Know what?" I asked, puzzled.

"We're staying at your place for the entire summer vacation!" Natasha declared.

"Really? That is amazing! Hurray!" I celebrated. This surprise was even better than the second one, which was also fantastic.

"Where are we going next?" I asked.

"Well, that's a surprise. Just follow my lead," Kyle said, much like a seasoned sailor guiding us through a tumultuous storm towards a welcoming lighthouse.

"For the first time, I began to appreciate the beauty of New York. The streets were perfectly laid out, and Green Avenue seemed meticulously planned. The sky exhibited a flawless shade of blue, adorned with clouds reminiscent of cotton candy drifting serenely. I was completely absorbed in this picturesque scene until my boisterous BFFs shook me out of my trance. Blinking in confusion, I asked, 'What's going on?' as they teased me about my behavior, which I denied, even though it was true."

Kyle took the lead, guiding us to a cutting-edge mini-internet café, which was the best I had ever seen. It boasted a range of modern appliances, from super ultra-chargers to hologram menus, robot waiters, and even complimentary MacBooks. I was left bewildered by New York's urbanization. Natasha teased me, saying, 'It seems like you're falling in love with New York now.' "The café' is impressive, but I'm not sold on the rest," I replied cheekily.

"Anyway, let's grab some coffee. Whenever I'm bored or need some peace of mind, I relax and watch the world pass by. So, I wanted you to experience that here as well," Kyle explained to us.

We indulged in coffee and pizza that melted in our mouths,

creating a heavenly sensation. Then, we captured countless memories on our phones, much to Kyle's dismay, as he wasn't a fan of lights and cameras. I posted a few photos on Instagram with the hashtag #BFFs, much to Kyle's chagrin. He complained about an unflattering photo, saying, "Why did you post that pic of mine? I asked you to delete that one; I look awkward there."

"Well, that's exactly why we posted it, buddy," Nats mocked, and I chuckled.

Curious about our next destination, I inquired cheerfully, possibly sounding chirpier than intended. Natasha remarked that I couldn't hide my newfound affection for New York. Despite my fondness for California, I had developed a liking for New York's stylish allure.

Suddenly, Natasha, with a burst of excitement, took the lead and announced we were headed to an iconic location. There was a playful disagreement between Nats and Kyle about the destination – the Statue of Liberty or Fashion Street.

"Whoopsies! I don't think it's a surprise anymore," I said, raising my brow teasingly. "Kyle! I told you the order," screamed Nats. "I forgot... sorry," said Kyle, scratching his head. "Thankfully, these two places aren't the last stops, though," he said absentmindedly, unaware that he revealed more about the tour.

"You know what, I am going to grab some tape and you know what's going to happen next, right?" asked Natasha, as though Kyle's death were confirmed. Kyle got frightened and just kept quiet. Natasha did have that impact on others but not on me. "So, where are we going then?" I asked. "Shopping!" squealed Nats. We both loved shopping no matter what. "I hope both of you are cool with each other," I asked. "Yeah, we are," said Nats, and Kyle heaved a sigh of relief. Natasha can be a little... (ok, fine! I must admit) no, very short-tempered.

It took about an hour and a half to reach Fashion Street even though we hired a cab! However, when we arrived, we were greeted by an enormous queue. Kyle and I were frustrated by the wait, but surprisingly, Natasha was not perturbed.

After a prolonged silence, she shattered the quiet with a bold proclamation. "Well, well, well... Are you two not disappointed that we journeyed all the way to Fashion Street only to face this crowd? It would have been exhilarating if we could bypass the line, but alas, such antics are forbidden. What if someone dared to take the chance? You both know who among us possesses the most daring and audacious spirit." Kyle and I sat in stunned silence, bewildered by her every word. With a fierce glare, she declared, "Moi, duh! I'm going to go ahead and cut the line!" Understanding her intent, we swiftly pursued her. "Hold on, Nats!" I shouted, urging her to halt this unethical endeavor, only to realize it was a prank when I spotted a special coupon in her hand. Though embarrassed, I resolved not to let it sour our plans.

Curious about the coupon, Kyle inquired, and Natasha explained that her cousin, who used to work there, had earned it for dedicating two years of hard work. These coupons not only allowed skipping the line but also offered discounts.

"No way!" I exclaimed.

"Yes, way!" affirmed Nats. "Let's hurry! We don't have all day, and we have loads to cover," urged Kyle.

I was captivated by the shop's entrance. It radiated an extreme funkiness with a life-sized mascot of a girl donning street attire and makeup. Clad in ripped jeans and a cap embellished with fake gems, she stood with crossed arms, exuding a boss-like aura.

Suddenly, the mascot approached me, scrutinizing my reaction. "Gah!" I shrieked.

"Relax, Shell. This is Maya, the mascot of Fashion Street," reassured Nats.

For those wondering, Fashion Street is a chain akin to H&M and Forever 21, not an actual street. However, it offers frugal prices and a trendier selection compared to other stores.

"What's up, girl?" asked the mascot.

"Nothing much…just here to shop," I replied with a nervous grin.

"Chillax!" said Kyle, "She's just a mascot, not a doll! She's alive and breathing." I sighed in relief, complimenting the mascot for resembling a doll.

As we entered the shop, an announcement blared over the intercom: today was a shopping spree, and the first to reach the billing counter without any items could grab at least five dresses for FREE!

"Oh, my flaming hot Cheetos, gosh!" exclaimed Kyle. But when he turned to look for us, we were already at the billing counter. In a flash, Kyle dashed over to join us. The three of us were ecstatic to be first in line, striking gold.

After about half an hour of shopping at Fashion Street, we had acquired more than five trendy outfits.

"Shall we go to the Statue of Liberty?" asked Kyle formally, and I could not control my laughter.

This time, we opted to walk instead of taking a cab as the

monument was nearby and cabs were expensive in New York. Upon reaching the top, I was fascinated by the bustling cityscape. The lady with the torch appeared mysterious.

"She's very creepy!" remarked Kyle, as though he were reading my mind.

We didn't linger too long at the Statue of Liberty but took a couple of photographs before continuing on our adventure.

"That was a day well spent!" remarked Natasha.

Well, readers, I may have bored you, but trust me, this is where it gets interesting.

Turning around, I was greeted by another captivating view. "What's that imposing monument? Why wasn't it part of our tour?" I wondered aloud, prompting laughter from Kyle and Natasha. Frustrated and eager for answers, I made the mistake of asking them again! Yet again, they guffawed even louder, and this time, I couldn't take it any longer. I fled the place without looking back.

"Geez! We were just kidding!" exclaimed Nats. "That's NOT a monument but the Mayor's house," explained Kyle. "To be honest, even I thought it was a historical palace until Kyle told me about it," said Natasha. "So, Kyle, do you know who the Mayor is?" I asked.

"Actually, I didn't pay much attention to that detail. I only came to New York a month ago," justified Kyle.

"Well, you should have," said a deep and gruff voice.

CHAPTER 3
Is that you?

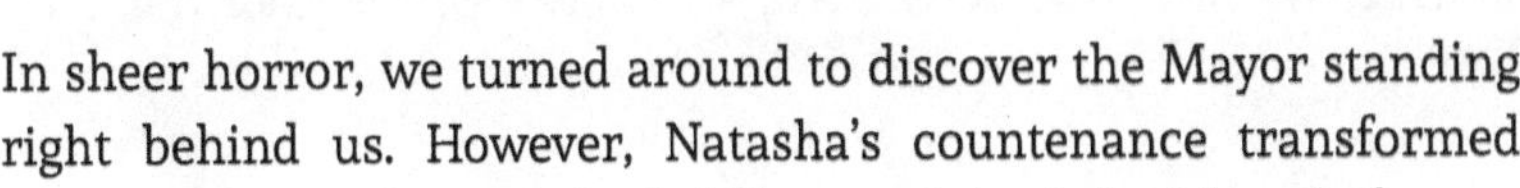

In sheer horror, we turned around to discover the Mayor standing right behind us. However, Natasha's countenance transformed into a warm smile, and she boldly scrutinized the Mayor's face.

"Guys, Mr. Williams is the Mayor of New York!" Nats exclaimed with enthusiasm.

Quickly realizing my blunder, I offered my apologies, "Oh, hello, Mr. Williams! I wasn't aware that you were the Mayor! I am sorry for behaving strangely."

Mr. Williams graciously responded, "It's fine! It's such a pleasant surprise to see the three of you here after so many years."

"So, Mr. Williams... Oops, Mayor," said Kyle, but the Mayor interjected, "No need to call me 'Mayor' all the time. My name is fine, plus, you three are like family, Kyle."

"Good to know, Mr. Williams," Kyle responded.

Curious about Mr. Williams' mayoral tenure, Kyle inquired, "How long have you been the Mayor? Is it a recent appointment, or have you held the position for a long time?"

Mr. Williams explained, "It's been a year now. A sudden interest in being involved in the governance of New York surged in my heart. I just wanted to take a break from running Cool Inc."

Surprised by this revelation, Nats chimed in, "OH! Cool Inc.? I thought you worked at Google. So, I guess you were the Mr. Williams associated with Cool Inc. whose name was published in the newspaper!"

Mr. Williams confirmed, "Yup, that's definitely me. After leaving Florida, we shifted to New York, and here's where Cool Inc. took birth."

Nats expressed her admiration for Cool Inc., declaring, "Cool Inc. is fantastic! It's the ultimate fashion hub! Why would you want to leave that?" Undoubtedly, there was a hint of disappointment in her tone. Mr. Williams, adopting a somber tone, responded, "Dear, it's difficult to comprehend the politics I was entangled in; however, I'll explain." He proceeded to recount the betrayal by a trusted advisor who temporarily seized control of the company, prompting Mr. Williams to labor tirelessly to regain ownership of Cool Inc.

"I faced numerous impediments and challenges during that period. In fact, all of this transpired just last year. The drama left me utterly drained, considering my age, you know. That rogue, on the other hand, despite being my age, possessed the energy of a twenty-year-old!" he sighed.

"You're not old! Please don't say that. Who was he, Mr. Williams, if you don't mind sharing?" I asked, brimming with curiosity. "I'm sorry, Shelly, but I can't divulge that. It's a sensitive matter. He ended up in prison, and his name has been expunged from all possible sources, websites, articles—you name it," Mr. Williams explained.

Kyle recognized the gravity of the situation, noting, "So, this was certainly not a trivial matter."

Mr. Williams nodded in agreement. I couldn't help but notice how significantly Mr. Williams had aged in the past five years, easily resembling a seventy-year-old. I remembered Mr. Williams as a youthful and free-spirited individual, but I couldn't overlook the marked transformation. I pondered how just five years could bring about such a noticeable change in one's appearance.

Mr. Williams broke the silence, revealing, "After my advisor got arrested, I no longer wanted to be a part of Cool Inc. and decided to take a gap year to see how the company fared without my direct leadership. The best part is that I still own the company, though I am no longer the CEO."

The Mayor then redirected the conversation, suggesting, "I hope you guys didn't forget about Kayla. You could meet her if you want." It was evident that he was uncomfortable discussing his advisor. Despite the tension, we agreed to meet Kayla and were escorted to her room by the guards.

"Kayla is here! This day keeps getting better and better!" exclaimed Kyle. But that wasn't the case for Nats. "I thought Kayla wasn't in New York" said Nats with a hint of dismay, noticeable only to her closest friends, Kyle and me. She had a past altercation with Kayla about five years ago just before Kayla left Florida for New York. I expected Nats to forget about that incident, but things don't leave her mind easily. They remain stuck in her mind like Super Glue.

"Sure, it's been ages! Yes, Mr. Williams, it goes without saying that we would love to meet our BFF," I said, hoping I hadn't gone over the top, but Natasha glared at me like a hyena.

"That's great! I know it's extremely late, and you might not have had dinner, but you still want to meet her. That's truly touching! You can have dinner at our place and come here as many times as you want," the Mayor said warmly. "Guards, please guide them towards Kayla's room," he requested. We bid farewell to Mr. Williams and followed the guards.

"Why the heck didn't both of you support me? You know what happened before Kayla left. We had a *humongogigantilarge* fight!" cried Nats.

"That's not even a word!" said Kyle.

"It doesn't matter! Couldn't you have mentioned that it was late, Shelly? Kyle is clueless, but you aren't," shouted Nats.

I stated firmly, "I did that on purpose, okay? For heaven's sake, both of you need to reconcile! It's been five years since your argument over a trivial matter, and you're still carrying it around in your minds!"

"But—" Nats began to respond, but Kyle interjected, saying, "Enough is enough! Let's go and reunite with our best friend without dwelling on those unpleasant memories. Natasha, I beg you to treat her with the same kindness and sweetness you show us. She loves you, and you love her too. You both used to be inseparable, and now it's our responsibility to mend things." I firmly grasped Natasha's left arm, while Kyle took hold of her right, and we forcefully dragged her. Our actions drew curious glances from the guards, who regarded us as though we were peculiar creatures. Despite feeling humiliated by their judgmental gazes, Natasha no longer resisted but let go of our hands and followed us with her head down. I mouthed a 'Thank You' to her, and she gave me a cold not-so-welcome look. We took the elevator after walking for about 10 meters. I was mesmerized by the vast splendor of Kayla's house.

I couldn't blame Nats for feeling awkward, as I shared the same sentiment. I found myself pondering whether Kayla had truly forgiven Nats and if our friendship could be fully restored. Eventually, I reassured myself by holding onto the belief that Kayla was good-natured.

We finally reached Kayla's floor, and the guards directed us to a magnificent door adorned with portraits of famous actresses. "Okay, that's weird... Kayla is into actresses now?" Kyle inquired.

"I guess not. Maybe she had nothing else to do and just stuck them on her door," I suggested.

"Meh! Who cares? Let's get this over with," Natasha said with indifference. One guard reached for the handle and informed Kayla, "Mistress, you have a few visitors."

Kayla remained unresponsive, not even bothering to turn around. It was evident that she was weary of frequent visitors at odd hours. "Let them in," she finally replied in an indolent tone. Though I couldn't see her face, I was certain she rolled her eyes. But I was confident that she would be overjoyed if she knew who her visitors were. We entered the bedroom, poised to surprise her.

"Surprise!" Kyle exclaimed enthusiastically, fully aligned with the plan.

"Surprise," Nats added, her tone less enthusiastic and avoiding eye contact.

Kayla turned back, and her reaction left us baffled. "Who are they?" she asked with a disgusted look.

"Wait, what just happened?" Kyle questioned.

"Told you..." Nats muttered.

"You don't know us?" I sarcastically inquired.

"Not a clue," Kayla replied, as though intending to mock us.

"She's just pulling our leg, I'm sure," said Kyle.

"I am not playing around. I seriously do not know who you urchins are," Kayla sternly replied.

"What has gotten into you? We are urchins now? Next thing you know, we will be non-existent for you!" Natasha opened her mouth and eyed her with murderous intent.

Frankly, I was unsure whether I was bewildered by her mannerisms or her appearance. She was a completely different person, like a new Kayla. She looked like a Barbie doll, except for her hair, which was auburn now, unlike her natural jet-black wavy tresses. The hairdresser had done a prodigious job with her hair, which looked as straight as a ruler. If I am not mistaken, she even got a nose job done. Her nose was no longer crooked but sharp and conical. Her eyes had an emerald hue, lined with kohl. Glitter was subtly added next to the corners of her eyes and a part of her cheeks. Her lips were pouted and sparkled with Maybelline lip gloss. She was dressed in an elegantly stitched gown adorned with fine floral prints and embroidery. It was both simple and stylish. But enough of her description.

I came up with a comeback and said, "So sorry for wasting your valuable time, Princess Kayla. We mistook you for our old friend. Please accept our apologies. I should have known that after seeing you. You see, our dear friend had a completely different appearance. She was socially awkward but had a heart of gold.

She used to be bullied at school until one day when we decided to support and befriend her. We wish we could meet her again, even just once."

"She exclaimed, 'I was never socially awkward! My life was teeming with popularity. I was never bullied... How could you?' asked Kayla.

'She was not talking about you. That was another Kayla. It is quite a common name, you know,' replied Nats.

'Stop the drama! I know you guys, but I was mortified to acknowledge you, and now that you know who I am...,' explained Kayla with a snobbish attitude.

'Yes, we knew exactly how you were; now, we don't. You have turned over a new leaf, and mind you, a very dark and crumpled leaf,' replied Nats.

Kayla's face broke into an astonished expression, with her mouth agape in terror, like the typical mean girl look. Kyle did not want to partake in the verbal scuffle as he had a long history with Kayla. There was pin-drop silence for a brief period until the desperate devil herself broke it. 'I don't know how well you remember me, but I was never like you all,' she pointed at us as though we were squirmy slugs, unworthy of her attention.

'You definitely were,' I said, taking out a picture of all of us from my pocket. That picture was so dear to me that I still preserved it securely. It was a picture of Kyle, Nats, Kayla, and me at Universal Studios. Those were the best of days. Kayla's eyes remained fixed, unblinking, for a whole minute. Her face turned pale, and her makeup dulled. I was not certain whether I imagined that last part or not, but clearly, she was shaken."

"She understood her mistake," Kyle whispered into our ears. Natasha shook her head in contrast. I did not want to hurt Kyle's feelings, so I gave him an appreciative nod. His face lit up, and he had a radiant smile. "Kayla, you there? So, how have you been doing? I hope everything is fine between us," asked an optimistic Kyle.

Kayla broke into a satirical guffaw and did not answer his questions. "Cut it out, nerd!" replied Nats.

To this, Kayla stopped laughing and became solemn. "There was nothing between us. Nothing that I remember of. Do not try to befriend me just because I am popular now, Kyle. We all were just friends, and I regret being yours. How could I have been associated with dorks! My younger self has never failed to amaze me, and she has done it yet again!" she said haughtily. Kyle was deeply hurt. His eyes had lost their bubbly sheen. The glow on his face vanished in the blink of an eye. Natasha fumed with rage. She couldn't stand seeing her best friends insulted. The circumstances were such that my pressure cooker released steam quicker than Nats', and I said, "Stop impersonating the cliché mean girls in high school! Do you realize that you've graduated high school, honey? You think you're too cool for school, but guess what? You're the complete opposite. Try being kind 'cause being cool isn't for you. I don't know why you think so highly of yourself, but you've got it all wrong."

"Wow! Give it a round of applause for Shelly and her eloquent discourse," replied Kayla, to which Nats clapped, and Kyle did too, albeit with hesitation.

To my shock, even the guards took her seriously and started applauding me. Kayla glared at them, and they stopped instantaneously. She turned red and cried, "Firstly, I'm not the 'cliché' mean girls' type. They were inspired by my swag. Secondly, everyone adores and reveres 'Moi' in the fashion industry. Lastly-" I never got to know what she was going to say as a fiery Natasha said, "It's pronounced as cliché and not 'clishay'! The only reason you were given the opportunity to be the face of cover magazines like Vogue and whatnot was because your father owns Cool Inc., and paid them heavily. Otherwise, you wouldn't have had any chance of making it big. You should really thank your stars, jerk!" Kayla was shell-shocked, and no words came out of her mouth.

Finally, she commanded, "Guards, remove these dorks from my sight and ensure they never return!"

"Better late than never, Mistress. We were puzzled by the amount of time you spent with them," replied one guard. Natasha shot him a withering 'I'll kill you if you don't shut up' look, and he immediately fell silent.

"This one is scary," muttered the second guard.

"The other one is kind of cute," the third guard commented while looking at me. I glared at him menacingly, but he didn't avert his gaze.

"Take them away quickly!" Kayla ordered. The guards clamped onto our arms with unyielding strength. I even attempted to bite one of their hands, but it was in vain. They wrestled us down the stairs instead of using the elevator.

"Release us!" I shouted.

"We'll report this to the Mayor!" threatened Natasha.

"Do whatever you want, but never return!" Kayla yelled back.

And that concluded our visit.

CHAPTER 4
Hooray! A party invite

"You don't have to physically kick us out of here!" Kyle screamed, finally finding his voice after the bizarre turn of events. Hardly had Kyle uttered these words when the guards were encouraged to push us further.

"An order is an order, twerp," one of the guards replied curtly. They left us humiliated at the entrance and hastily closed the gate.

"Is this even legal?" I inquired, surprised by the lack of response from the guards.

"It's already 10!" Kyle exclaimed, breaking the tense silence.

"Were we there that long? It felt like only a minute or two," replied Nats as we quickly got to our feet.

"Mrs. Peterson will be worried," Kyle thought aloud.

"More than that, I'm concerned about her temper!" I exclaimed. We exchanged no further words as I booked an Uber, expecting it to arrive in a minute or two. Unfortunately, luck was not on our side. Despite the cab's arrival, it took us a whole hour to reach home. It seemed that something was amiss in my life yet again.

Upon reaching home, my mom wore the same expression and

posture as the day of my arrival. I gritted my teeth with anxiety and began recounting the details of our tour and the reason for our lateness. Since my friends were there, she did not want to show her frightening side and urged us to freshen up quickly.

"You see, your mom understood the situation, Shelly," Kyle reassured.

"You'll never get it, will you?" I replied in a frustrated tone. The chat with Kayla was perfectly vile, and it drained all the energy from my body. I truly do not know how Natasha handles such situations with ease.

After freshening up, we gathered for dinner. I recounted the entire adventure from beginning to end, including the minor details I had skipped earlier. My mom listened attentively, and surprisingly, she was not shocked by Kayla's attitude.

"Well, I knew that the Mayor was Kayla's dad, but I had no idea about her changed personality. She is not a prominent figure in this neighborhood. One can only spot her entering a black limo and speeding through the streets. She is always travelling and rarely stays at her place. Show me a picture of her. Has she changed, or is she still the same little girl with long, black plaits?" asked Mom.

Nats responded with a contemptuous smirk, a clear indication that I had made a big mistake by asking her to apologize to Kayla. "We do not have a picture of her, but you can easily find one on Google by typing 'Kayla Williams'," replied Kyle with pride, still showing signs of lingering feelings for Kayla despite her recent behavior with him.

Mom decided to look up Kayla online, and her eyes widened to the point where I worried, they might pop out of their sockets.

"What happened to that angel? She is like those plastic girls we despise! Henry is not like that. How did he let his daughter go down this path? This is so unlike him, very unlike him..." muttered Mom. I do not blame her for feeling like that. Imagine having a close friend whom you have not seen for five years, and when you finally reunite, they have turned into a completely different person. I empathized with her and did not want to belittle her feelings.

Kyle was the only one who seemed forgiving of Kayla's behavior, choosing to overlook her harsh words. "She was not so bad, Mrs. Peterson. Maybe she is still upset about the fight with Natasha," Kyle suggested. Nats disagreed, saying, "She is not dwelling on that, Kyle. If that were the case, she would have simply ignored me and talked to both of you. But that wasn't the case, was it? What about her outfit and taste in fashion? She has changed for the worse."

"Stop the bickering, y'all! Leave that snob. Have dinner now or else all my hard work will be wasted," Mom urged. I dug into Mom's Italian cuisine without further ado. The exotic red sauce pasta melted in my mouth. I wondered if paradise tasted like that. Kyle enjoyed the Lasagna, but Nats seemed distant and uninterested in the food.

"Nats, what's up?" I asked, noticing her lack of appetite. Natasha did not respond immediately, seemingly lost in thought. "Nats?" Kyle asked, trying to draw her attention.

"Oh, so sorry. I was engrossed in eating. Dinner is splendid, Mrs. Peterson!" exclaimed Nats, snapping back to the present moment.

"Thank you, dear," replied Mom. Kyle and I exchanged a glance, silently acknowledging the tension surrounding Natasha's behavior. Indeed, she did harbor the desire to reconcile, despite her outward demeanor suggesting otherwise.

Why did Kayla have to change? Everything could have been so perfect! Four best friends reuniting after five long years—it's the stuff of dreams. But dwelling on what could have been won't change the harsh reality staring us in the face. Sadly, there's no way to rescue Kayla from herself now.

As we finished our dinner, we headed for the bedroom. Kyle hit the sack within a minute or two, exhaustion finally catching up to him. Nats also dozed off within ten minutes, her troubled thoughts seemingly pacified by sleep. However, I found myself restless, unable to shake off the events of the day.

Somehow, sleep eluded me, and I tossed and turned in bed. Natasha, in her sleep, growled at me, a habit of hers that never failed to startle me. Left with nothing else to do, I turned my gaze towards the window, where the stars twinkled in the dark night sky, offering a silent solace amidst the chaos of my thoughts.

Was I distressed by Kayla's behavior? I quickly tried to brush off that trivial matter. After an hour or so, I fell asleep. The next day, Kyle screamed in my ears to startle me. I gave him a slap on the cheek and my mom screamed at me. What a way to begin the day, right? Nats did not participate in the morning rants; she simply chuckled. The morning was uneventful; I just went with the regular morning drill. This time, Mom prepared Natasha's favorite dish, Chicago-style pizza. Nats could not wait and immediately sat down to munch on the crispy pizza.

"Mrs. Peterson, you are a brilliant chef! That was better than the one I had in Chicago!" Nats praised. Mom blushed and replied, "Stop it, dear! I am not such a great chef." Once we were done, Nats, Kyle, and I contemplated what to do next. We ran out of options, but Mom had a solution to keep us occupied.

"I will introduce you to the members of my community welfare group. You kids will finally get to know about the background work that goes into maintaining a neighborhood," she suggested. "Nay! We will give it a pass, Mrs. Peterson," Kyle replied. "Kyle, this was not expected from you, dear. I thought that Shelly would oppose this," Mom said, sounding disappointed. Kyle became sheepish and did not look Mom in the eye. To make him feel better, I chimed in, "Mom, that's such a boring idea! He isn't incorrect." Natasha expressed, "I am cool with it. I have no issues in conversing with total strangers about a neighborhood whose name I did not know until now."

"That is the spirit, kiddos! Now, dress up quickly as I have a meeting with them in half an hour," replied Mom. Kyle and I glowered at Natasha for what she had done. Nats gave us an equally puzzled look, but she seemed to be wistful. "She does not pick up on sarcasm, does she? Or perhaps she does but pretends not to understand it," I whispered. Astonishingly, Nats seemed to get the gist of what I meant. Mom went into her room to change for the meeting, but the three of us did not feel the need to change our clothes, thinking we were dressed appropriately—neither too shabby nor too formal.

"Guys, do you remember what tomorrow is?" I asked. "National Junk Food Day?" guessed Kyle. "I can't believe you forgot it!" exclaimed Nats. "Neither can I. It is Kayla's 22nd Birthday!" I reminded him. "Oh, yeah... It slipped my mind," explained Kyle. Nats and I exchanged knowing looks; it was evident that he pretended to forget her birthday to cope with his hurt feelings. After Mom came out of her room, she urged us to follow her. On our way to the meeting, we unexpectedly bumped into Mr. Williams once again! He greeted us with a wide-toothed grin, which felt awkward to reciprocate given his daughter's misbehavior.

"How do you do, Grace? Hello, kids!" Mr. Williams greeted us. I was astounded to see Mom blush a little. Was something brewing between them? Had Mom chosen not to disclose it to me? Several questions swirled in my head, but I put on a pleasant expression and greeted the Mayor.

"I am fine, Henry, just the usual. My daughter, Shelly, has come to visit me. Kyle and Natasha came to surprise her," Mom responded. "I met them yesterday. They have grown so much, more handsome, and prettier. Why didn't you stay for dinner?" the Mayor asked. Natasha was about to give a savage reply when I cut in.

"If we had lingered any longer, Mom would have made mincemeat of us," I explained, making a chopping motion with my hand. The Mayor burst into laughter and could not contain himself. Mom shot me a 'wait and watch what will happen at home' look. My expression briefly changed to terror, but thankfully, it was not noticeable.

"Oh, I almost forgot! Here you go," he said, handing over a neatly sealed envelope. "What's this for?" I asked. "It's for Kayla's twenty-second birthday tomorrow. I figured, why not invite her best friends!" he replied. "What a fantastic idea!" Kyle chimed in instantly. Nats was dumbfounded. She had no intention of engaging with Kayla again and might not even want to see her.

"Thank you for the invitation, Mr. Williams!" I said courteously. Mr. Williams began conversing with Mom on the neighborhood and her duties. Nats was determined not to go and stood apart from us. Was she plotting something? I warned her not to stir up trouble. She responded that she could not guarantee that. I was annoyed but I decided to drop the subject. After a while, the conversation seemed to have ended and we said our goodbyes.

"Uhm... Mom? None of us really wants to go to Kayla's party. Is it okay if we skip it?" I asked.

"Are you out of your mind?" cried Mom. "There's no way around it unless you are fine with hurting the Mayor's feelings," she added.

"We shall go, Mrs. Peterson. I'll make sure these two attend with me," Kyle said, stepping in to ease the tension.

"Thank you, dear," Mom replied, relieved to have his support. "Natasha and Shelly, please adjust just for a day. I know she is no longer your best friend, but please pretend to have forgotten about last night's incident. I don't think Henry knows about what happened yesterday. He is a gentleman, you see. He'll be humiliated and distraught if he found out...Just let this one slide," Mom pleaded, her tone softening with concern.

"Okay, fine!" I said with a sigh, conceding to my mother's plea. Natasha didn't respond; she simply ran away, leaving us bewildered by her sudden departure.

"Nats!" Kyle yelled, his voice echoing with urgency. "We have to follow her!" I cried, already feeling the weight of worry settling in.

Mom got worried and was about to sprint after us, but I reassured her that we could handle it. Never in my life had I witnessed Natasha flee from a situation. Something was going on, but I couldn't quite read her emotions. I knew her so well that I could usually predict her every move, much like looking into a mirror.

"Phew! I can't figure this one out," I admitted, feeling a mix of frustration and concern swirling within me. Kyle urged, "What are you waiting for? Let's hurry!"

I nodded in agreement, determined to uncover the mystery behind Natasha's sudden behavior. "Come back soon! I will not be here as I'll be attending a meeting at Mr. Williams' place," yelled Mom, her voice tinged with worry and a hint of resignation. "Got it!" we said in unison, as we rushed off to find Natasha, uncertain of what awaited us. Nats, here we come!

CHAPTER 5

It's none of your business!

"How did she manage to dash past us without us even noticing?" I inquired, puzzled by Natasha's sudden disappearance. Kyle shrugged in response, his brows furrowed in confusion. "I have no idea," he admitted.

" 'Cause she has mastered the art of parkour," a voice chimed in from behind us. Startled, Kyle and I turned around to see Natasha grinning mischievously.

"Sup, losers! You can't keep up with me," teased Nats, her tone playful yet tinged with a hint of underlying emotion. She wasn't bluffing; she effortlessly leaped over various obstacles, displaying a level of agility that left us in awe. At one point, we almost lost sight of her amidst the bustling surroundings. She seemed like a real-life action movie heroine, akin to the Avengers.

"Shelly, hurry!" yelled Kyle, his voice filled with urgency as we struggled to keep pace with Nats.

"Coming! Don't wait for me; keep going! I'll catch up," I replied, trying to keep up with their swift movements. However, as we continued our pursuit, I couldn't shake off the feeling that we were going in circles. It dawned on me that we were on a wild goose chase, futilely attempting to catch up with Nats' elusive figure.

Finally, I spotted a shadow to my left and recognized it as Nats'. With a hint of sarcasm, I quipped, "Well, well, well, if it isn't Natasha Noel."

Nats didn't respond; she remained hidden behind a pole, although she knew her shadow was visible. There was pin-drop silence for a few seconds, punctuated only by the sounds of our heavy breathing.

"Nats?" I asked empathetically, sensing that something was amiss. I noticed water droplets splattering where Nats had been standing. Was she crying? Without waiting for her to reply, I rushed over to her, concern etched on my face.

"Why are you crying? What's wrong?" I asked, gently placing a hand on her shoulder to offer comfort.

Upon hearing this, Nats emerged from her hiding spot, her expression initially blank but quickly morphing into an amused look as she gazed at me. "Someone spilled water from the apartment above. Why would I cry? You know I'm not like that," she explained between chuckles.

"But you are human too, Nats, and it's okay to admit when you're not fine. The strongest people are the ones who acknowledge they're not okay," I quoted, hoping to offer her some comfort.

Nats quizzically inquired, "Was that an inspirational quote?" To which I replied with a half-smile, "I hope it helped."

Turning to my left, I noticed Kyle, clearly fatigued from our chase. "Nats, you're incredibly agile. You should teach me parkour," he suggested with a grin.

Nats responded with a gentle smile, acknowledging his compliment.

Curiosity piqued, I asked, "So, why did you run?"

Nats paused for a moment before replying, "So that I could have a private discussion with both of you about..."

"About Kayla?" Kyle interjected; his interest evident.

"Who else could it be?" I responded with a wry smile. "I just wanted to emphasize that my decision not to attend her party doesn't mean you both are obligated to do the same. You can go if you'd like," Nats assured, her sincerity shining through.

"Really?" Kyle asked, his eyes lighting up with hope.

But I couldn't let him entertain false hope. "No, that's not right. 'All for one and one for all' has always been our motto. If Nats isn't going, we won't go, Kyle. Don't be selfish. Please let go of any hopes of reconciling with her. You are no longer her type, and she doesn't deserve a kind-hearted person like you," I asserted firmly, surprised by the sudden eloquence of my words.

"But, how can you be sure of that? Maybe she was simply in a bad mood?" Kyle tried to defend the situation. I retorted, "Oh, come on." Then, Nats' eyes lit up, and I realized that this was her 'Eureka' moment.

"Kai-Kai, don't be disheartened. I've decided to give Kay-Kay a chance," Nats responded. She was addressing Kyle with a cute nickname and referred to Kayla as Kay-Kay! Something was up, so I decided to wait and watch.

"That's amazing, Nats!" Kyle exclaimed and hugged her. "Please, go ahead," I encouraged. Innocently, Kyle questioned, "Why are you acting as if Nats has hatched a plan and telling her to continue?" I couldn't help but wonder how Kyle managed college without us, given his naiveté. I furrowed my brow as I looked at Nats, and finally, she let the cat out of the bag.

"Since I am willing to meet Kayla tomorrow, let's purchase a gift for her together. I took the initiative to scout for some stores, which is why I had you running all over, Kyle," Nats explained. "Oh, really?" Kyle responded, as he shyly scratched his head. The poor guy still liked Kayla and was blind to her changed personality. Kyle continued walking ahead of us toward the closest gift shop.

"Do you intend to give her the worst gift possible?" I interjected. Nats' eyes widened in astonishment. "How did you.." Nats began to say, but I cut in, " Something that would remind her of the past or perhaps even insult her?" Nats remained silent, flabbergasted that I had discerned her intentions. "You do understand me inside out," Nats retorted with a smirk. "I have known about your complex personality since childhood. But I won't let you. We can either choose not to attend or go and select a thoughtful gift. I don't want to embarrass Mr. Williams. Seeking revenge may seem tempting, Nats, but it's not the right path. The choice is yours," I stated, then walked past her, following Kyle's lead.

Nats grunted in frustration and hurried after me. Kyle meticulously studied every object in the gift shop. "How about this lantern?" he suggested. "That's pretty cool! But is it suitable for a 22-year old's birthday?" I wondered. "Yeah, you're right. Let's look for something better," he agreed. "Oh, what about this cobra statue?" Nats proposed. "Nats, no one would like to be gifted an ominous snake that would scare the bejesus out of them!" Kyle replied. "Huh! So, you weren't listening to me after all!" I scoffed at Nats.

"Kyle, she is a brave woman. Something like that won't frighten her. It's just a statue," Nats defended her choice. Kyle and I exchanged eye rolls in response to her argument, and Nats eventually gave in, pretending to search for a more suitable gift. "Ta-da! A witchcraft set!" Nats announced. "How did you come up with something so quickly?" Kyle inquired. Nats flexed and beamed with pride, her eyes closed. "She's not a child, Natasha!" I reprimanded. "But she's a witch, Shelly," Nats retorted.

"Not gonna happen," Kyle replied as he placed the box back on the shelf. He returned to us, carrying a large white plush teddy bear with adorable black beady eyes. This time, Nats rejected the gift. "Seriously, Kyle? A teddy bear? Why are you so stereotypical?" asked Nats. "Girls like teddy bears, right?" asked a clueless Kyle. "You just don't get it, and you've proven it. Not a teddy bear," I responded.

"Is it a gift for Ms. Williams?" asked a croaking voice. Even before I turned to look at the speaker, I knew it was an elderly woman. "Yes, Ma'am," Kyle replied politely. "Are you Kayla's grandmother?" Nats inquired. Instead of answering, the old lady posed another question. "Are you planning to gift this to her? I would not recommend that," she advised.

Kyle looked crestfallen, and she added insult to injury. "Even the cobra statue and the witchcraft game were better," she remarked.

Was she stalking us? Had she been watching us this entire time? That's quite unsettling.

"Well said, Granny!" said Nats offering her knuckle for a fist bump, but the stern woman declined. Nats didn't appreciate her attitude and walked away grumpily.

"I suggest all of you leave this gift shop right away and head to a boutique. Getting something for her here is a bootless errand. The spoiled brat won't appreciate anything, no matter how expensive," she advised.

I wasn't attentive to what she was saying because I had stumbled upon something perfect for Kayla. "Guys, I've found the best thing ever!" I exclaimed, presenting them with a fashionable gown.

Not only was it a sleek piece of clothing, but it also bore a meaningful quote embroidered on it: 'You are braver than you believe, stronger than you seem, and smarter than you think,' a testament to the words of wisdom from A.A. Milne. Kyle was ecstatic about the gown. 'It's perfect!' he exclaimed.

"Nats?" I asked.

"Why does my opinion even matter to the two of you?" she sighed.

"Very well, then, it's settled," I concluded.

"The fact that her father owns the world's best fashion brand means she'll never appreciate such a simple gown," the old lady commented.

"It's not solely about the beauty of the dress. The quote on it is beautiful, and I'm confident she doesn't have a dress like this," I said confidently.

"Suit yourself," replied the old lady before making her way towards the store exit.

"Who are you?" asked Kyle.

"That's something for you to figure out," she said, closing the door behind her.

"She's quite mysterious," Kyle observed.

"Why can't the old hag just mind her own business!" Nats grumbled.

"Nats, please don't call her that! After all, she's older than us," Kyle cautioned.

"But she seemed to know Kayla pretty well. Maybe she's related to her," I speculated.

We purchased the dress and opted for it to be gift-wrapped.

"It will fit her, right?" Nats asked, hoping to avoid giving her the gown.

"Hundo P!" replied Kyle with a thumbs-up and a wide, toothy grin.

"I know her behavior was HORRENDOUS, but we are the good guys! We can't stoop to that level," I commented.

"How can you be so forgiving, Shelly, after all that she did to us? How can you forgive her? How?" Nats inquired.

"We must be the bigger person, Natasha," I replied calmly.

Nats seemed to sober down a bit, understanding my perspective.

"It's already noon! Shelly's mom must be waiting for us," said Kyle.

"Can we go a little later? I am not in the mood to socialize with the elders in the Community Welfare group. Mrs. Peterson wanted to introduce us to them," Nats expressed.

"That sounds good!" Kyle replied as he changed his mind.

"We must leave now! I got rebuked last time and I don't want a repeat," I requested.

"Just this one time," Kyle negotiated.

"Thanks!" I said, and we made our way to the Mayor's house. We reached the same spot in about half an hour, but my Mom was nowhere to be seen.

"Are you looking for someone?" asked Mom.

"Gah!" I let out a shriek. She was standing right behind me. "Mom! You scared the hell out of me," I reacted. Thankfully, she was in a pleasant mood and not vexed.

"Actually, we arrived before Mrs. Peterson, Shelly. That's why she was behind you," Kyle blurted out.

"Kyle, you naughty twirp!" yelled Mom. "Sorry, Mrs. Peterson. Please forgive me. But am I correct?" Kyle asked.

"Yes," Mom reluctantly agreed. "Ha ha! He caught you, Mrs. Peterson," replied Nats.

"Why did you run away, Natasha?" Mom inquired.

"Simply," replied Nats with a casual shrug. Kyle was amazed by her laid-back personality. Nats had two sides to her - sometimes she could be savage, and other times, she was cool.

"At least we managed to avoid the intros," Kyle said, relieved.

"What introductions?" asked Mom.

"Nothing," Nats quickly replied as she covered Kyle's mouth and dragged him out of Mom's sight. "We are heading home, Mrs. Peterson!" Nats announced.

"Wait for us!" Mom called out, but they had already left.

"Oh, I totally forgot! You have to meet my Welfare team," Mom reminded me.

"Can we skip that, Mom?" I asked with pleading eyes.

Fortunately, Mom fell for it and said, "Well, if not today, you'll have to meet them tomorrow because they are also invited to Kayla's party."

"What? Why would Kayla invite them?" I wondered.

"The Mayor is in charge of the guest list, not Kayla, even though it's her birthday," Mom explained.

"Oh, I see. How many people are invited?" I asked.

"About forty, if I'm not wrong," said Mom.

"Only forty? I thought there would be at least a HUNDRED!" I exclaimed.

"Only the elite are invited to her party. However, Henry wanted to invite the Welfare team as well," Mom clarified.

"We've already bought a gift for her, Mom," I informed her.

"I thought I would take care of that, honestly," Mom responded.

"No worries, we've got it covered," I assured her.

"Did Natasha agree to go?" asked Mom.

"Well, not exactly, but I'm sure she will," I replied.

"Did they run away from me to avoid interacting with my team?" Mom asked.

I chuckled and admitted, "Yes!" "We also encountered a peculiar elderly lady who was quite inquisitive. Do you happen to know anyone like that?" I asked.

"Dear, there are many elderly women in Green Avenue," Mom responded.

"Let's get going! Kyle and Nats are waiting for us," I cut in.

"You'll be fine, right?" asked Mom.

"Don't worry, Mom. I can handle Kayla," I reassured her.

"I'm more worried about Kyle than Natasha, Shelly," Mom said.

"That is indeed worrisome, but I'll make sure he doesn't get hurt by that girl," I promised.

"Great! You are an angel, Shelly," said Mom.

I hugged her, and we headed back home.

CHAPTER 6
Too extravagant! Ugh!

"Polka dots or stripes?" asked Nats.

"I'd go with stripes," I replied.

"Nah! Polka dots," Kyle responded.

"Sorry, Kyle, but this is girl-to-girl," Nats explained.

"Whatever, just don't regret your choice," Kyle replied.

Nats seemed a bit hesitant after his comment. "Are you sure, Shell?" she asked me.

"You are seriously considering Kyle's choice?" I asked, and he raised his eyebrows, smiling.

"No," replied Nats. "Stripes, it is!" she affirmed. She held the dress against herself to see if stripes suited her.

"If you wear polka dots, it might look like you have meatballs all over your dress," I jested.

"Hey!" Nats retorted.

"What will you wear, Shell?" asked Nats.

I went to my closet and retrieved a body-hugging dress with a metallic sheen. "Now, that's what you call party wear!" remarked Kyle.

"Isn't mine as well?" Nats inquired.

"He's just playing with you," I reassured her. "Anyway, I'm wearing this!" said Kyle presenting a tuxedo.

"A tuxedo!" Nats and I exclaimed.

"Yes, why not?" he questioned.

"Wear something more casual," Nats suggested.

"It's not a wedding, and you look a bit too mature," I added.

"Guys wear tuxedos to parties," Kyle defended his choice.

"Don't be that guy," Nats advised.

"Show us your other clothes," I insisted.

He brought his suitcase over to us, and Nats went through his clothes. After studying about ten different items, her eyes settled on a black jacket and a white top. "This, along with jeans, is the perfect combo!" Nats declared.

"Bravo, well done, Nats," I praised.

"Okay, fine!" Kyle agreed.

"We are all set with what we are wearing. Now, what's the next part?" Nats asked with a sly grin.

"Wait, is there more?" Kyle asked with wide eyes.

"Knowing Nats, there's always more," I replied.

"Yo, I'm going to Kayla's party, giving her a decent gift, and you expect me to act like a saint to her?" Nats questioned, placing her hands on her hips.

Kyle was about to respond, but I intervened. "What's on your mind now, Nats?" I asked with frustration.

"We're going to play a prank on her and sabotage her party," Nats revealed, accompanied by an evil laugh.

"Come on, don't be a child! We're adults," I rebuked her.

"But how?" Kyle inquired with surprise, ignoring what I said.

Nats whispered something into his ear.

"Aren't you going to tell me?" I asked.

"Well, Shelly, you don't like hurting others even when they do the same to your best friends," Nats replied.

"Leave it, then. You can proceed with whatever you have planned," I replied. In reality, I was seething with anger because of Kayla. I was simply testing whether Nats was as upset with her as I was, pretending to be forgiving to see her reaction.

"Well, guess what? I pulled off a prank on Nats!" I declared.

"I knew it!" replied Kyle. He did? When did he become so clever?

"What prank?" Nats asked.

I explained in detail about impersonating a saintly person.

"Shell, I knew it! You may be forgiving, but when someone crosses the line and hurts your friends, you will never forgive them," said Nats.

"Yes, but I still don't want you to be rude to her. Playing a prank is fine," I said.

"Tell me the plan," I insisted.

Nats described the entire prank. I realized that she was a mastermind!

"That's too harsh for her," Kyle remarked.

"This is quite mild," Nats countered.

"But will it work, though?" I questioned.

Nats smiled and gave me a thumbs up.

"What are you planning?" asked Mom suddenly.

When did she enter the room? Was she eavesdropping?

Kyle replied, "Uh, nothing. We aren't planning any sabotage or anything of that sort."

"Nothing, Mom. We just decided what we'll wear," I covered.

"I am heading for my meeting now. Don't worry, I'll be back in half an hour and then we can attend the party," Mom informed.

"Okay, then. Bye!" we said.

"You guys are acting weird. Is something going on?" she asked.

"Nothing!" I said so loudly that Mom glared at me.

"Why are you repeating the word 'nothing' all the time?" suspected Mom.

"For no specific reason, Mrs. Peterson," Nats coolly replied.

"I am going then. Take care, kiddos," she said and left the house.

"Phew!" Kyle muttered.

"Kyle! Why did you break into a cold sweat?" asked Nats.

"I dunno! It always happens when I'm planning something secretly," Kyle justified.

"We could have been caught!" I yelled.

"It won't happen next time," guaranteed Kyle.

"It better not," I said.

"Let's get going, then! The party is in an hour and we haven't got dressed," Nats urged.

"You're right. Mom has already worn her party wear and is attending her meeting in it," I explained.

I carefully ironed my shimmery dress, while Nats worked on transforming Kyle's look into something more impressive. She did a surprisingly good job.

After forty-five minutes, we were all done with our makeup and were all set for the party. Mom rang the doorbell, and I hurried to open it.

"You're late, Mom!" I grumbled.

"So sorry, dear," said Mom apologetically.

"Woah, the three of you look like a million dollars!" Mom complimented.

"Thank you, Mrs. Peterson," said Kyle shyly.

"We'd better get going!" I urged.

"Right," Mom agreed and closed the door.

We rushed to the Mayor's house to make it on time. To our surprise, there was a queue ahead of us.

"Phew! We aren't late, I guess," said Mom with a sigh of relief.

"Why is there a security check?" asked a gullible Kyle.

"For the security of the Mayor," Mom explained seriously.

"Did something happen to the previous Mayor?" Nats asked, her interest piqued.

"No, dear, nothing like that. There was just a small incident a long time ago. It's just that the crime rate in New York is remarkably high, as you know," justified Mom.

"What happened earlier?" I cut in, but Mom's expression turned into a furious one, so I decided to stay quiet. It seemed like she was getting fed up with our questions. Thankfully, Nats had my back and changed the subject.

"By the way, are any college students invited to Kayla's birthday? Someone our age?" asked Nats.

"Uhm... Let me think. Oh, yes! Her boyfriend is your age or maybe a year older," Mom replied.

"Say what?" Kyle was dumbfounded, shocked to learn that Kayla had moved on.

"Couldn't you hear what I said, Kyle? Should we take you to the ENT?" Mom asked with concern.

"No, Mom. That's just a rhetorical question to express amazement," I clarified.

"Oh, okay. Kids these days! Their slang changes so fast, it's hard to keep up. It'll take a while to catch up," Mom remarked as she kept an eye on the queue. My gaze fell upon the lady in front of us, the same old lady we encountered in the gift shop the other day. The security guard conducted a thorough full-body scan on her with a millimeter-wave machine. For some reason, the old lady appeared uneasy, which only added to her enigmatic personality.

"Could you please remove the small bottle from your left pocket and hand it over to us?" the guard requested.

"That's very precise. Very well," the old lady complied, fetching the bottle from the left pocket of her skirt. The guard scrutinized the bottle as though it were an explosive, turning it upside down and inspecting it from every angle to assess its contents.

"What exactly is in this?" the guard interrogated.

"Oh, boy! This is going to take a long time," Kyle remarked.

"Shut up, kid!" the old lady snapped.

"He's not wrong, miss. You must cooperate with us and do as we say. There are many people behind you," the guard sternly reminded her.

"This is my medicine for asthma. You can check the list of contents on the label," she explained.

Still unconvinced, the guard opened the bottle and sniffed it carefully, like a curious dog trying to discern its contents.

"Let me have a look at it," another guard interjected.

"Yes, Sir," the first guard acquiesced, handing him the bottle. The second guard sniffed it and read the contents.

"Do you have severe asthma?" he inquired.

"Not always. It happened only once. But the doctor advised me to keep it handy," she clarified.

"How come it has such a strong odor?" questioned the first guard.

"That's the normal odor for such medicines. My dad was a severe asthma patient and had the same syrup," she explained.

"Oh, I see. Sorry for the delay," apologized the first guard.

The old lady didn't respond and instead glared at the first guard for portraying her as the bad guy.

"What a rigorous check!" exclaimed Kyle.

"She was suspicious. I don't blame the guard for that," Nats smirked and added.

Mom chimed in, saying, "Every arcane old lady isn't necessarily a criminal."

"That's true," I agreed.

"Next!" yelled the first guard, seemingly frustrated with his earlier suspicion. Kyle hurried forward to complete his turn swiftly, while I followed and went through astonishingly fast without any issues. Mom was next and passed the inspection without trouble.

Nats, being the last in line, engaged in a conversation with the guard about the previous incident. "Maybe you were right, Sir. That must have been poison," Nats speculated.

The guard was about to reply when Kyle interrupted, "Natasha, we don't have time. We're already late!"

"Urgh! I'll meet you on the way out. Sayonara!" Nats said as she took leave of him.

"Hey! You should've let me talk to him. What if there's a crime?" asked Nats.

"Did Shelly tell you about a crime recently?" asked Kyle.

"Not at all! Just because I read detective novels doesn't mean I'll talk to people about crimes!" Nats stated.

"It pretty much means that," Kyle retorted.

"Let's get going!" intervened Mom, urging us to move along. We got frightened by her tone and kept mum.

There were two more guards at the doors to the Mayor's house. Security was top-notch here! We had to present our invitations to the guards, and after all the checks, we were finally allowed into the party. Loud party music filled the air as we entered. The celebration was already in full swing, and most of the guests had already arrived. It didn't take long to spot the birthday girl, who was only a few meters in front of us. She was engaged in conversation with a charming young man who appeared to be around our age.

His wavy hazel-brown hair was neatly swept to one side, and his eyes had a lively orangish-brown sheen. He exuded an amiable charm and wore an elegant suit with a perfectly tied tie. A Rolex watch adorned his right wrist, suggesting he hailed from an elite background. He had an alluring smile, revealing pearly white teeth, much like famous actors in the movies. My mother nudged me to keep moving.

"Wait, Mom. She's talking to someone important," I explained.

"How do you know he's important? Is it because of his striking looks?" asked Mom.

For no apparent reason, I began blushing, which only confirmed Mom's point.

"Go ahead, kiddos," urged Mom, pushing us forward.

"Happy Birthday, Kayla!" Kyle shouted before we could hand over the gift to her.

Kayla seemed embarrassed by Kyle's presence and softly replied, "Thank you," without even looking at us to avoid further interaction.

Nats was taken aback by Kayla's outfit, which was quite unusual. She was wearing a gamer girl's suit, with a myriad shade of black and purple and geometrical designs all over.

The funniest part was the tiara on her head.

"Are you into gaming?" asked Nats.

"I am into a lot of things, and gaming is one of them," Kayla replied haughtily.

"Are you on Twitch?" I asked, being a gamer myself.

"Duh! Why wouldn't I be on Twitch? It's the main site for us gamers," she responded.

"What's your favorite game, then?" asked Kyle.

"Fortnite," she answered.

"Did you participate in the Champion's league last week?" asked Kyle.

Kayla hesitated but finally said, "Yes, I did."

"How did it go?" asked Kyle.

"Uhm... it went well," she said with hesitation.

"What was-" Kyle began to ask when she quickly averted his

question and said, "I'm sorry, I have to greet the other guests."

"No problem," I replied.

Kayla then turned to Eric, the young man she had been speaking to earlier, and asked if he wanted to join her. He declined, saying, "You can go on. I'll stay back."

"Hi, we are Kayla's old friends, and you are?" asked Nats, trying to break the ice.

"Oh, hi! I'm Eric, as you heard from her," he replied with a pleasant smile.

"How are you related to her?" I asked.

"I'm her boyfriend," he revealed.

Kyle boiled with rage from the inside but looked calm on the outside. He was good at hiding his feelings from others."

Nice to meet you," I said to ease the tension.

"Are you in college as well?" asked Nats.

"I never went to college. I'm a model, you see," he explained.

"Wow, that's cool!" I exclaimed.

"Thanks," he replied modestly. It was no wonder Kayla chose him; he was her type.

"I gotta go now, but before that, I couldn't catch your names," he said.

"I'm Natasha, this is Shelly, and that's Kyle," Nats introduced.

"It was great meeting you all, Shelly, Natasha, and Kyle," he reciprocated.

"Goodbye!" we said, and he waved and left.

"Oh, so you met her boyfriend. I overheard your conversation," remarked Mom.

"Mom, Kyle is here. Can you please not?" I asked.

"Oh, I'm sorry! So, what do you think of this place?" asked Mom.

"It's too extravagant! There are thousands of chandeliers all over the ceiling, and the lights are blindingly bright!" complained Nats.

"I agree!" I added.

"But it's beautiful, right, Kyle?" Mom asked.

"Yeah," he replied, in an impassive mood.

"Did she like the gift?" asked Mom, breaking the silence.

"Oh, shoot! We totally forgot about that," I admitted with a sense of urgency creeping in.

"Hurry before it's too late," urged Mom, a hint of worry in her voice.

"She's that way!" said Mom, pointing in Kayla's direction with surprising precision.

"Wow, Mrs. Peterson! That was quick!" Nats remarked, impressed by Mom's keen observation skills.

"She has a knack for spotting things," I added, sharing a smile with Mom.

Mom grinned, and once again nudged us forward, her attention diverted by her friends calling out to her.

"Where are you going, Mrs. Peterson?" inquired Kyle, curiosity evident in his voice.

"To meet Henry," she replied, her plans momentarily interrupted by her friends' unexpected arrival.

"Grace, there you are!" exclaimed a lady about Mom's age. "Hey Trina! Hi, everyone!" replied Mom as she went along with them.

"I hope she likes it," said Kyle, his fingers crossed in anticipation.

"She will, but knowing her, she won't readily accept it," stated Nats matter-of-factly, her practicality shining through.

"Don't worry, Kyle. Just chillax! I'm sure she'll love it!" I cheerfully reassured him, trying to lift his spirits.

"Thanks, Shell," he said, visibly relieved by my words of encouragement.

This time, Kayla wasn't with Eric but with another girl who seemed like one of the 'mean girls' straight out of the movie "Mean Girls."

"Hey, Kayla! We totally forgot to give you your gift! Here you go!" I said, handing over the wrapped dress with a hopeful smile.

Kayla eagerly opened the gift, but her reaction was not what we expected. Both she and her friend broke into a guffaw, much to our dismay.

"What's the matter?" asked a troubled Kyle, his expression a mix of confusion and concern.

"Seriously, you chose this?" asked Kayla, her bemusement evident in her tone.

"Even my little sister has better fashion taste than that," her friend chimed in, adding insult to injury.

"Who are you, Mrs. Snobby?" retorted Nats, unable to contain her frustration.

"How dare you call me that! You don't know who I am? I'm Hayley Queen!" she replied indignantly, expecting recognition for her name.

None of us reacted to her identity, which left Hayley even more startled and irked by our nonchalance.

"Never heard of your name," I replied casually, dismissing her attempt at intimidation.

"But you must be Kayla's sidekick, for sure," Nats added, unfazed by Hayley's attempts to assert her superiority.

"You!" growled Hayley, her annoyance evident as she clenched her fists in frustration.

"It's a simple dress, but the quote changes everything," Kyle explained, trying to salvage the situation.

"Which quote?" asked a puzzled Kayla, her curiosity piqued.

"It's literally in the center of the dress!" pointed out Nats, urging her to take a closer look.

Kayla read the quote at the center of the dress, kept quiet for a moment, and finally said, "You bought this dress for a stupid quote?" Her dismissive remark made Nats see red.

"Do you even know how to read? It's such a powerful and inspirational quote, and you treat it like just a bunch of letters!" shouted Nats, defending her choice vehemently.

"We models don't wear such tacky clothes!" replied Hayley with a dismissive gesture, adding fuel to the fire.

"Why were you so well-behaved with us when Eric was there?" I questioned, curious about her sudden change in demeanor.

"I didn't want him to know that I hate you guys! He considers me an angel, and angels don't hate anyone," she replied snobbishly, her true colors showing through.

"Leave her, Kyle. We shouldn't care when people like her don't appreciate such gifts," said Nats as she pulled him away, refusing to let Hayley's negativity ruin their day.

Even I didn't bother to turn back; I went to look for Mom, feeling disheartened by Kayla's reaction. It had been a bad day for Kyle. Firstly, Kayla had replaced him with an extremely successful model, and now, she pretended to detest our gift, adding insult to injury.

"Don't pay heed to her opinion, Kyle," I comforted him, trying to lift his spirits amidst the disappointment.

"How can I not? I thought we could get back together, but now, she doesn't even like my taste, unlike earlier times. Every time I try to do something to impress her, I always fail," he lamented, his disappointment palpable.

"Now, she has a much better boyfriend who cares for her and is a thousand times more dignified than me! I don't know what to do! I'm helpless!" lamented Kyle in frustration, his voice tinged with defeat.

"It's simple! You must move on! She doesn't deserve someone like you, and you don't deserve such a horrible person like Kayla! You are kind, sweet, and much more caring. You never hurt her!" replied Nats firmly, her words laced with conviction.

"It's not a cakewalk for me, Nats! I have tried many times, but I just can't fight that feeling!" he admitted, his vulnerability laid bare.

"We can fight it together! Don't think about her and focus on tonight! We have a party to enjoy! Let's dance and have some snacks. Party mode: ON!" I exclaimed, trying to inject some positivity into the situation.

Kyle started smiling after hearing my pep talk, and we headed over to have some snacks. A helper attended to us and offered appetizers, which turned out to be extremely spicy.

"I need water! Water!" cried Nats, her reaction exaggerated yet genuine. Kyle and I couldn't contain our laughter at her animated response, nearly doubling over with mirth.

"On the way, mistress!" replied the flustered helper, eager to rectify his mistake and avoid a scolding from his boss for making the dish too spicy.

After a while, Nats calmed down as she drank about a liter of water to soothe the spiciness on her tongue.

"You should not bite into the chili, Nats!" Kyle quipped, gently teasing her. Nats unwittingly did a commendable job of diverting his mind from Kayla.

"Wait, that was a chili! I mistook it for a bell pepper!" she said, realization dawning upon her with a sheepish grin.

"Where's Mr. Williams?" wondered Kyle, noticing the absence of our elderly acquaintance.

"Dunno! Let's ask Mrs. Peterson," Nats suggested, looking around for our chaperone.

"He must be busy with paperwork," replied a voice from behind us, startling us all.

"Sassy granny!" exclaimed Nats, her irreverent streak shining through.

"Don't call me that!" retorted the old lady, her tone sharp.

"What should we call you then?" asked Kyle, intrigued by her mysterious demeanor.

"Call me Ma'am," she said, asserting her preference.

"Ma'am! Not that! Why can't you reveal your name?" I asked, curious about her reluctance to disclose her identity.

"I... don't want to," she replied cryptically, maintaining her air of mystery.

"Do you know that I suspected you during the security check? Now, you're acting even more suspicious, Sassy Granny," said Nats, unable to resist a jest.

"Did you suspect an innocent old lady?" she inquired, her voice tinged with offense.

"Well, you aren't even disclosing your name! So… yeah, I don't think someone innocent would be afraid to do that," Nats retorted, adding fuel to the fire.

"You nasty girl!" scowled the old lady.

"So, did she like it?" she asked, turning the conversation to Kayla and the dress.

"What?" asked Kyle, confused.

"That Kayla girl and that dress," replied Sassy Granny.

"Oh, about that. Can you not?" I asked, stepping in to protect Kyle.

"I knew it! She loathed it, right?" asked Sassy Granny, cutting right to the point.

I nodded in agreement. None of us expected an old lady to deliver an "I told you so," but she did just that.

"I told you so! Always listen to your elders because they're much more experienced than you youngsters," she gloated.

"Can you not rub it in? Kyle's already terribly upset," I said, trying to ease the tension.

"Oh! Really? I wasn't aware of that. I'm sorry, dear," replied Sassy Granny, surprising us with her softer side.

"It's not a big deal, Granny. You didn't know, and it is all on me for not listening to my close friends. Sorry for being such a knucklehead, Shelly and Nats," said Kyle, taking responsibility.

"Come on, man! You don't need to say 'Please, Sorry, and Thank you' to your BFFs! Otherwise, we wouldn't even be friends," Nats quipped.

"Sassy Granny... my apologies, Granny, did you happen to see the Mayor?" I asked, changing the subject.

"Mayor Williams seems to be tied up with some official matter. I'm sure he'll come for the cake cutting," said Sassy Granny.

"Speak of the devil, here he is!" announced Kyle.

"Hey kiddos! Apologies for the blunder of not greeting the guests. That's totally on me and not on my responsibilities. I wasn't even doing much. Just whiling away time in deep thought on how to improve the landscape of our neighborhood. As you might have noticed, New York as a city has never been green. I have drafted the perfect plan to implement my strategy," the Mayor explained.

"Why are you working on your daughter's birthday? Shouldn't you be on leave?" asked Kyle.

"Dear, the Mayor has to work all the time and he shouldn't be a slacker. No matter what, I can't shake off the duties. Moreover, I'll be present for the cake cutting, and her Mom will be there till then," he added.

"Oh, we totally forgot about Mrs. Williams! How's she doing?" asked a jovial Nats.

Natasha had a deep fondness for Mrs. Williams. They would gel together seamlessly, like bread and butter, black and white... you get the idea, right, readers? Mrs. Williams was the only person who provided moral support to Nats in her aspiration to become a fashion designer. She even convinced Nats' parents to take full responsibility for Nat's future.

"About that... how should I word it? Uhmm..." hesitated the Mayor.

"Did you get?" asked Nats, her apprehension palpable.

"Hope and I got divorced," said the Mayor at last.

"I'm so sorry!" Kyle and I replied in unison. I was apprehensive about Nats' reaction, expecting her to erupt in anger at Mr. Williams. However, to my surprise, she remained calm.

"She didn't even tell me about this. She assisted and advised me despite experiencing this! When did this happen?" questioned Nats, her curiosity piqued.

"A year ago," confirmed the Mayor.

"A year?!" cried Nats, visibly stunned. "I thought it happened recently, like a month ago. Who's Kayla's stepmom?" she asked, her tone shifting to that of an inquisitive mother-in-law.

"She's Juliette, a famous Fashionista. She isn't Kayla's stepmom yet, as she's my fiancée," he answered.

"Juliette as in, the Juliette Clover!" I exclaimed with excitement.

"Yes, that's her," he replied, confirming my excitement.

"Where is she?" asked Kyle.

"Right over there," he said, pointing towards the dance floor.

"I thought that was a young girl," remarked Nats.

"She does look like one from that angle," chuckled the Mayor.

"I have to get going. I didn't even see Kayla this entire day. I might forget her face soon," he quipped, earning a laugh from Nats.

"Nice one, Mr. Williams! Up top!" cried Nats, prompting a high-five from the Mayor.

"See, Sassy Granny! You should return a high-five when someone gestures one!" explained Nats, referring to the old lady, who had slipped away unnoticed.

When did she leave? She was as stealthy as a cat even at that age.

Kyle remarked, half-jokingly, "Sometimes I wonder if she's a witch!"

"Lydia left when I arrived. She isn't a big fan of mine as the Mayor. In fact, she blatantly asked me why I was chosen as the Mayor. She moved in right after the elections were conducted," he replied.

"Lydia, is it? Sassy Granny has finally been named! Why didn't she reveal it earlier, though?" wondered Nats.

"She has always been secretive. It's not new for anyone who knows Lydia. 'A lone wolf' is a better term for it," he explained.

"I must go! Bye, Kiddos!" he bid us farewell.

"We aren't children anymore!" I protested.

"But for us adults, you'll still be! Where's Grace?" he asked before leaving.

Nats and Kyle exchanged knowing looks, and I shot them a glare.

"Oh, she went along with her friends in that direction," I gestured with my hand.

"Thanks! I'll catch up with you guys for the cake-cutting," he said before departing.

"Goodbye!" we responded in unison.

"Is something going on between... you know who and the other?" asked Nats with a cheeky smile.

"Do you mean between Mr. Williams and Mrs. Peterson? Grace and Henry... Grenry!" quipped Kyle.

"Stop shipping them! They're just good friends who happen to be in the same Neighborhood Welfare group! Plus, he's with Juliette," I interjected firmly.

"That's for you to believe, not for them, and he wanted to meet her before Juliette," replied Kyle.

"Okay, let's move on. How about dancing?" I suggested.

"Shelly wants to dance? I thought you didn't," asked Nats, surprised.

"Since we are at a party, we might as well," Kyle supported my idea.

"That makes sense... What are you waiting for? Let's go!" Nats agreed enthusiastically.

The dance floor pulsated with energy as Mom and her friends took center stage, showcasing surprisingly impressive moves for their age. Professional dancers captivated the crowd with their skilled performances, executing daring stunts that left the audience in awe. Amidst this spectacle stood Juliette, a vision of elegance in her flowing white gown adorned with sparkling pearls. Her perfectly tousled bun accentuated her youthful appearance, complemented by a tiara adorned with delicate doves. Juliette's slender figure effortlessly carried any outfit, exuding grace and sophistication. With subtle pink lip gloss and a natural glow, she defied the expectations of a typical fashionista by opting for minimal makeup, radiating beauty from within as she danced with infectious joy.

"Juliette! Juliette Clover! Can I have an autograph, please?" bellowed Kyle, his voice echoing like a loudspeaker, drawing attention from everyone on the dance floor.

"Security! I've spotted a fan attempting to mob me and invade my privacy!" Juliette exclaimed, prompting swift action from the guards who escorted us away, dashing our hopes of joining the dance.

"Kyle, you moron! I was really looking forward to dancing, and I had planned a secret prank!" scolded Nats, her frustration evident. Even I felt disappointed, realizing my own covert mission to spy on Mom and Henry had been thwarted. Could they be secretly dating without my knowledge? The thought gnawed at me, despite my efforts to dismiss it. "Henry is not a bad guy, but I didn't want to live with Kayla!" Why are these irrational thoughts plaguing me? Lost in my reverie, Kyle's voice brought me back to reality. "Shelly, I hope you aren't mad at me for this. You couldn't get to spy on them because of what I did," he confessed, his words breaking through my inner turmoil.

"Spy on whom?" I innocently inquired, though my mind raced with the implications.

"Don't act dumb, Shell. You know exactly what we're talking about, but I'll explain it anyway. It's about Grenry!" Nats replied jovially.

"No... Why would you think that?" I attempted to deflect, but my face betrayed me, breaking into my infamous shy grin with my eyes closed. Nats and Kyle weren't fooled this time; they easily saw through my crystal-clear expressions.

"It's the Shy-Face Shelly!" they both declared simultaneously.

"No, no, no!" I denied their allegations, though my protests fell on deaf ears.

"You wanted to spy on them!" Nats accused, to which I shook my head, but they refused to believe otherwise. Eventually, I succumbed to persistent curiosity and revealed my plan.

"Ah, I see...." Kyle remarked with an annoying smile.

"Can we leave this topic now? It's done and dusted!" I implored them, and they agreed to drop the subject, ceasing their pestering. We decided to hang out near the drinks counter and dance cautiously, making sure not to accidentally knock over any drinks or draw the attention of the guards.

"Come to think of it, don't you think we've had some bad experiences with the security guards here?" Kyle commented.

"I never really thought about it, but I guess you're right," I replied with a laugh. Surprisingly, Nats didn't seem to react to Kyle's joke and remained silent.

"Nats? Nats?" Kyle called her. "Oh, I'm sorry! What were you talking about? I was just thinking about what a strange character Sassy Granny is. She could easily fit into a detective novel. If I were the detective, Lydia would be a suspect," she mused.

"Give the old lady a break!" said Kyle sympathetically.

"You called me an old lady, Kyle?" asked Mom, with astonishment.

"No, not you, Mrs. Peterson. It was for-" Kyle began explaining, but I quickly jumped in and said, "Mom! There you are!"

"Hey, kiddos! I didn't see you on the dance floor. What's the story?" Mom inquired.

"Um... let's just say, I happened to shout out to Ms. Clover, and then the guards prohibited us from dancing ever again," Kyle reluctantly confessed.

"Uff! All for that snobby lady!" Mom sighed, facepalming.

"Exactly, Mrs. Peterson!" Nats echoed.

"But she's a good person. She is very kind and sweet," Kyle defended Juliette.

"If that's the case, why did she behave so meanly with a fan?" asked Nats, highlighting Juliette's overreaction.

"Why are both of you so against her?" I questioned.

"Because she's the reason Hope, sorry, Mrs. Williams couldn't become a fashionista or a model," explained Nats.

"Mrs. Williams had a shot?" asked a baffled Kyle.

"Yes, she did! In fact, she was always better than Juliette, but the only issue was that Hope never knew how to play politics. Juliette outdid her in that and claimed a spot!" Nats informed us.

"I didn't know that!" said Mom with a gasp.

"Neither did we," replied Kyle and me.

"Anyways, kiddos, these are my friends. The most awaited meeting, right, Kiddos?" Mom said, trying to change the subject.

"Yeah..." we said, hesitating and giving a sheepish smile.

"Hey, this is Trina!" she introduced us to her friends.

"I'm Jade, and that's Courtney," Jade added.

"Hi! I'm Shelly, Grace's daughter, and those are my BFFs, Kyle and Natasha," I introduced us.

"Hello, ladies! Nice to meet you! You can also call me Nats," Nats chimed in.

After the Hi's and Hello's were done, Mom asked her friends to describe the work they were doing. Honestly, none of us were even paying attention. In fact, Kyle even unintentionally yawned and quickly apologized for it.

"I don't blame you, Kyle," I whispered to him.

I recalled Jade mentioning that she was the head of the Welfare Squad. To keep the conversation flowing and avoid an awkward silence, Kyle asked, "How many members are there in your squad? Is it only the four of you?"

"Yes, dear. We kept it a small group for more efficiency," replied Trina with enthusiasm.

"Ladies, I really need to use the washroom! I'm so sorry!" Mom suddenly announced.

"It's okay. It was great meeting the three of you. You guys are exactly how Grace described you to be," said Jade.

"What did she say about us? More importantly, what about me? If you forgot me, my name is Nats," Nats interjected.

The ladies broke into hearty laughter and complimented Nats for her natural talent for humor.

"She praised you, Nats. Anyways, see you later," said Trina as they left hurriedly. Courtney and Jade also took their leave.

"I wonder what Mom ate that made her rush to the washroom," I pondered aloud.

"Maybe it was those hot appetizers. I didn't like them either. Sweet people have a sweet tooth whereas others don't," joked Nats.

"Which way did she go? Maybe she has diarrhea," suggested Kyle.

"I hope not! She gets very weak during those," I added with a concerned frown.

Just as we were about to set off in search of Mom, one of the waiters approached us, holding a tray of masks.

"What are these for?" asked Nats, her curiosity piqued.

"Ms. Kayla loves masquerade balls. We're asking our guests to wear masks for the masquerade; it'll make it a challenge to recognize people you know," explained the waiter with a polite smile.

"Ah, I see! That's quite exciting!" I remarked, intrigued by the idea.

"I'll choose the green one," declared Kyle, already reaching for his preferred mask.

"Hey! I had my eye on that one!" I protested playfully.

"Don't worry! We have plenty more masks," the waiter assured me with a grin.

"No, it's fine, really. I was just pulling his leg. I'll go for the hot pink one!" I decided with a smile.

"Hmm...there are so many funky options here. I think the neon orange mask is the funkiest," remarked Nats, examining the selection.

"Thank you for your prompt selections," said the waiter courteously before leaving to attend to other guests.

"Now, where were we? Oh yes, Mom!" I remembered suddenly.

"I think she went towards the north," suggested Kyle, pointing in one direction.

"Nah! I think she went the other way," countered Nats, pointing in the opposite direction.

"I bet you didn't even pay attention to where Mrs. Peterson went! You just want to disagree with me," accused Kyle with a playful smirk.

"Relax, Kyle! Now's not the time for arguments! We need to find Mom. She should be out of the bathroom by now, unless she's still in there because of... you know," I said, expressing my concern.

Nats and Kyle fell silent, realizing the urgency of the situation. We quickly headed off in the direction we thought Mom might have gone, but before we could get far, we were once again interrupted by someone!

CHAPTER 7
The Calm before the Storm

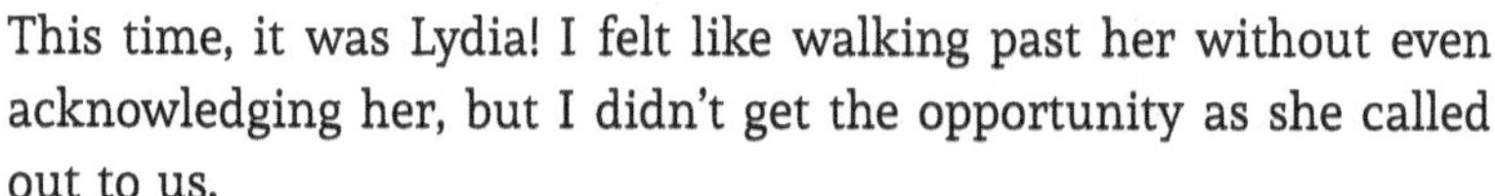

This time, it was Lydia! I felt like walking past her without even acknowledging her, but I didn't get the opportunity as she called out to us.

"What are the Three Musketeers up to again?" she asked in a satirical tone.

"Nothing much. Just looking for someone," Kyle replied.

"We know all about your identity! You're Lydia and are approximately eighty-six years old. You are a very secretive person, you hate Mr. Williams, and you're known to be a lone wolf," Nats stated, as if she had conducted deep research on Lydia and had uncovered these facts.

Lydia was stupefied and exasperated. "You nasty brat! I'm not even seventy! In fact, my age is the opposite of what you said! I'm sixty-eight not eighty-six! Don't you have any manners? You're talking to an adult, remember that, Nasty Natasha!" she retorted.

Nats was so taken aback that her mouth was still agape. "Excuse me, Ms. Lydia! I consider you a fun pal! Pals can talk to each other like that, Sassy Granny," explained Nats.

"Well, I don't consider you a pal," Lydia replied, causing Nats' eyes to bulge like those of a toad.

"Anyways, see you later, Sassy-. Sorry, Lydia!" said Kyle. Even Kyle was on the verge of calling her Sassy Granny. To keep the narrative entertaining and comical, I might refer to her as Sassy Granny, but "Lydia" is much shorter, so I'll stick with that.

"Searching for Grace, eh?" Lydia suspected.

"How did you-?" I began to ask when she interrupted, "That way!" and pointed to the south.

"Thanks!" I replied and ran ahead of Kyle and Nats.

"Told you, Kyle! It was south!" Nats said, raising her eyebrows.

"I'm sure you guessed it, but in the end, I was wrong," Kyle admitted.

The masquerade ball was lively and bustling! Everyone was wearing a mask, and the waiter was not wrong. I couldn't recognize a soul, not even Princess Kayla. But after some time, I spotted her because she had donned the fanciest mask. It was golden in color and adorned with beautiful sequins, leaves, and feather decorations, making her stand out in the crowd.

We went south and knocked on the door, but Mom wasn't there. A helpful waiter informed us that there were four bathrooms available for the guests: one situated in the north, south, east, and west directions.

"There are an abundance of bathrooms, but they're quite far apart!" exclaimed Kyle.

"We have no choice," Nats said with a shrug.

"She's right. It's obvious we'll have to knock on all of them," I remarked.

We knocked on every door, and our repeated interruptions seemed to irk most of the people inside.

Eventually, thanks to Murphy's law, we located Mom in the northernmost bathroom. It struck us as rather odd to have four bathrooms for guests that were so far apart.

When we knocked and called for Mom, she replied, "Hey, kiddos! This will take some time! I checked all the bathrooms until I reached this one, which happened to be unoccupied."

"Mom, are you feeling alright?" I asked.

"I think I'm experiencing some indigestion," she replied.

"Is it diarrhea? Do you need any help?" I asked, expressing concern.

"I'll be out in a while," she assured.

"But you didn't answer my question," I insisted.

"I'll be out in a while," she repeated.

"We're going!" Kyle declared.

"I'll be out in a while," Mom replied once more, her attention seeming elsewhere. With her behavior growing increasingly peculiar, we opted to leave, granting her some privacy.

"See, Nats! I was right! Lydia just wanted to make us run around, so she misled you about Mrs. Peterson heading south," Kyle explained.

"Fine, whatever," Nats replied with an eye roll.

After walking for about ten minutes, we returned to the spot where we had encountered Lydia.

"She vanished into thin air!" Kyle commented.

"Typical of her, nothing out of the ordinary," I responded.

"Let's try on our masks! I'm curious to see how we look!" Nats suggested.

I examined my hot pink feline mask, complete with adorable whiskers and cat ears. "I didn't realize yours was a cat!" Nats remarked upon noticing my mask.

"Neither did I," I replied.

"Mine is simply a mask. The light green shade perfectly matches the color of poison," Kyle commented.

"Now, we won't have to worry about the guards. They won't be able to identify us with these masks," Nats explained.

"That's purrfect!" I quipped.

"There you are!" Mom exclaimed as we approached.

"Oh, you're back. Are you feeling better, Mrs. Peterson?" Kyle inquired.

"Much better. I think it was those spicy starters that didn't suit me," Mom responded.

"I told you!" said Nats, clearly reveling in her favorite line.

"Why are all of you wearing masks?" Mom asked, puzzled.

"Oh, about that... a waiter approached us and offered a selection of masks for the masquerade ball," Nats explained.

"I need a mask as well," Mom announced decisively before darting off to find the waiter, leaving us in her wake.

Navigating through the vibrant throngs, we entered the dance floor, now enchantingly transformed into a masquerade ballroom. Much to our relief, the ever-watchful guards remained oblivious to our presence, granting us passage into the heart of the festivities. For what felt like an eternity, we surrendered ourselves to the rhythm, dancing ceaselessly until fatigue overcame us, leaving us sprawled on the floor, utterly spent. Only Nats remained indefatigable, her energy seemingly boundless as she continued to dance without pause. Amidst the revelry, she captured moments with her camera, immortalizing us adorned in our masks."

"Nats, take a break!" Kyle implored, gasping for breath.

"I don't get tired so easily. Where's Sassy Granny Lydia?" Nats asked.

"Why are you constantly fixated on her?" I asked, my curiosity getting the better of me.

"I can't explain it. There's just something about her that gives me the creeps. She's not like everyone else; I'm sure of it. Whenever I see her, I sense she's hiding something," Nats responded.

"Speaking of which, Lydia hasn't vanished. She's right over there," I interjected, gesturing to the northwest. Lydia stood out as the sole individual at the party not donning a mask.

"What a killjoy! She's not even embracing the spirit of the ball," Kyle remarked.

"Well, she is elderly, after all," Nats reasoned.

"Everyone, please gather for the birthday girl's cake cutting!" a voice announced over the loudspeakers.

"It's already nine!" exclaimed Kyle, checking the time after what seemed like ages.

"Time truly flies, doesn't it?" I remarked.

Kayla's excitement peaked, and she couldn't contain herself any longer for the cake cutting. However, just as she was about to blow out the candle, she paused and declared, "I won't do this without Dad. Juliette, could you please ask him to drop whatever he's doing and come downstairs?" She requested politely.

"Where are you off to, Nats?" I inquired.

"I'm just grabbing a glass of wine. I'm twenty-two, so it's perfectly legal for me," Nats replied.

"We completely forgot about the prank!" I suddenly realized.

"Oh no! We'll have to do it after the cake cutting," Nats replied before heading to the drinks section. We knew managing her after she'd had a few drinks would be quite the challenge. She was already a bit unpredictable when sober, so we dreaded to imagine what chaos she might unleash with even a sip; trouble would surely follow! I'm not exaggerating, dear readers.

Meanwhile, Kyle and I waited for Mr. Williams to arrive for the cake cutting. Juliette had gone upstairs to fetch him. It seemed he was exceptionally busy because he hadn't even made an appearance at the masquerade ball. I cursed my luck when Nats returned with not one, but two glasses of wine.

"Why two? Is the other one for one of us?" I asked.

"Nope, they're both for me to savor!" Nats joked.

"When do you guys plan to have it? Would you like some?" she offered.

"We'll have it after dinner," Kyle replied, speaking for both of us.

"Where's Mr. Williams?" Nats inquired.

"Not sure. Juliette went to fetch him. She should be back any moment now," I replied.

Juliette rushed down the stairs in a panic, her hands trembling, her face drained of color, and her eyes telling a tale of shock all their own. Seeing her distress, Kayla asked, "Where's Dad?" her concern evident in her voice.

Juliette hesitated before finally managing to say, "Your father... he's... gone." Her words trailed off as tears streamed down her cheeks.

"What!" Nats exclaimed before anyone else could react. The glass of wine in her hand slipped from her grasp, shattering into a mosaic of clear crystals on the floor, surrounded by spilled red wine.

CHAPTER 8
The lines in front of us

Kayla stood frozen, her emotions too tumultuous to muster even a reprimand for Nats, who had carelessly shattered expensive kitchenware. Tears streamed down her face, blurring the lines of her meticulously applied makeup. Eric reached out to comfort her, his gentle pats on her shoulder offering solace, but Kayla abruptly left the dining room, her destination clear: she sought solace, perhaps one last glimpse of her beloved father.

The guests were perplexed, their murmurs filling the room as they speculated on the unfolding situation. Some, like Mom, found themselves speechless initially, only to succumb to tears as emotions overwhelmed them. Kyle, known for his penchant for drama, wept openly, his tears genuine and uncontainable. Nats and I, though deeply upset by the events, remained strangely dry-eyed, our emotions roiling within us despite the absence of visible tears.

The ballroom buzzed with chaos as whispers and speculations swirled around the sudden demise of the Mayor.

"How can we be sure he's truly gone? Perhaps Juliette overlooked something in her assessment? She's not exactly known for her attention to detail," Nats ventured in an attempt to offer consolation.

"I... I don't believe that!" Kyle's sorrowful cry echoed through the room, tears streaming down his cheeks unchecked.

"I can't help but consider the possibilities. If indeed he passed away, was it due to natural causes, or could foul play be involved?" I pondered aloud.

"I can't bear to entertain such thoughts," he replied, his voice choked with emotion as he blew his nose into a tissue.

"I had a nagging feeling that today might unfold in this manner. Even during the security check... I can't shake the suspicion that Lydia may be involved," Nats suggested.

"I'm not so sure. She's an elderly woman; orchestrating something like that seems beyond her capabilities," I countered.

"But what about that peculiar syrup she had with her? One of the guards even suspected it might be poison," Nats added, fueling our apprehensions further.

"The other guard inspected it thoroughly and found nothing amiss. What's crucial now is determining the cause of the Mayor's death. Mr. Williams was a gentle soul, and his absence will be deeply felt," I remarked solemnly.

"I'll miss him too. And if I ever discover who's responsible for his death, they'll pay dearly!" Nats exclaimed, her voice filled with righteous anger.

After a few minutes passed, Kayla and Juliette descended the staircase, their appearances reflecting the turmoil within. Makeup streaked their faces, and Kayla had changed into comfortable attire, signaling her disinterest in the festivities. Eric approached Kayla, but she turned away, silently requesting some space.

Meanwhile, Juliette engaged in a serious conversation with Jade, who nodded in understanding, indicating that she had been entrusted with a task.

Lydia stood slightly apart from the group, visibly distressed yet choosing to conceal her emotions behind a tissue. With determined steps, she moved towards the main gate of the Mayor's house, but her departure was halted as Jade addressed the gathering.

"Please, remain in the ballroom," Jade's authoritative voice rang out. "Ms. Clover has alerted the authorities for a thorough investigation into the incident. All guests will be questioned, but rest assured, no one will be deemed guilty without concrete evidence. Stay calm and cooperative."

"It appears he was murdered," I remarked, a sense of unease settling over me.

"But with all the guards present? It seems improbable," Kyle countered, his disbelief evident.

"It is possible. The security check may have been compromised. Perhaps one of the guards overlooked suspicious or hazardous items, just like with the syrup incident," Nats pointed out.

"STOP! Let's not jump to conclusions. We can inquire with Juliette whether poisoning or stabbing was involved," Kyle proposed.

"Agreed. Shall we approach her?" I suggested, eager to unravel the mystery surrounding the Mayor's untimely demise.

Nats and Kyle nodded in agreement, and together we approached Jade. "Jade, could we have a moment?" I requested.

"Of course, but I'm pressed for time. Juliette needs my assistance with contacts," she replied hurriedly.

"Understood. Can you tell us if the Mayor was stabbed or killed by other means?" Kyle inquired.

"I'm not entirely certain, and I don't believe it's necessary to disclose such details to the guests. However, since you're affiliated with Grace, I'll share with you confidentially," Jade confided.

"We're unsure of his condition at the moment, but truth be told, the outlook doesn't seem promising," Jade informed us. "We'll need to await confirmation from the doctors regarding his status. More details about the incident will surface during the investigation, but let's refrain from spreading panic. While he wasn't stabbed per se, Juliette mentioned a significant incision in his skin."

"That's distressing news. Thank you for sharing, Jade," I expressed my gratitude.

"It's no trouble, but please maintain a sense of surprise when the news breaks," Jade added.

"Should we inform Mrs. Peterson?" Nats asked.

"She's already been informed. I just spoke with her. Please, take care of Grace. She was deeply attached to Henry and must be shattered," Jade revealed.

"We will," I assured her. After our conversation with Jade, we searched for Mom.

"Mom! I'm so sorry!" I exclaimed, rushing to embrace her.

"Oh, Shelly! How could such a tragedy befall him? Who could

have harmed dear Henry?" Mom lamented, her tears flowing uncontrollably once more.

"We understand your pain, Mrs. Peterson. There's still hope that he may be alive, so please don't lose faith and continue to pray for him. Rest assured, the perpetrator will be apprehended and brought to justice soon," Kyle reassured her, his voice filled with compassion.

"I hope so. But what if they escape justice for such a heinous act? Oh, Henry!!" Mom's voice cracked as she sank to the floor, her tears flowing ceaselessly. It was heart-wrenching to witness her anguish.

"The culprit must answer for their actions! To harm someone so dear to my mom... I can't bear it any longer! Kyle, Nats, we must take matters into our own hands and launch our own investigation!" I declared, determined to seek justice for Henry and console my grieving mother.

"An investigation? Can we pull it off? Are we capable of such a task? And what if he's still alive?" Kyle questioned, voicing doubts and concerns.

"You're right, he might be alive, and perhaps our lack of formal training could be an advantage. We might just be better than them. We're not bound by bureaucratic red tape like real detectives. We can rely on our instincts and quick thinking. We don't have to waste time on paperwork. And hey, Kyle may not be the sharpest tool in the shed, but he has his strengths. We can assign him a role that plays to his strengths, like documenting witness responses," Nats encouraged us with her inspiring words.

Kyle's face lit up with newfound enthusiasm, momentarily forgetting the sorrow of the Mayor's fate. However, his optimism was short-lived as the wailing sirens of two police vehicles pierced the air.

"Well, that was quick!" I remarked, noting the swift response of the authorities.

The police officers rushed through the gates and entered the ballroom, blocking Lydia's path as she attempted to leave.

"Everyone, stay where you are! You three, keep an eye on the guests. Ben and I will head upstairs!" commanded the burly cop, who appeared to be in charge, addressing his team.

"Poor Kayla must be distraught!" I whispered to my friends.

"Absolutely. It's unbelievable that a murder was attempted during a party! When you think about it, parties create an ideal environment for such incidents with the loud music and distractions of the guests. Everyone is preoccupied, making it easy for a perpetrator to exploit the chaos," Nats reasoned. Who wouldn't make hay while the sun shines?" she added.

"That does make sense," Kyle concurred.

"Juliette, Kayla, and the cops are coming! Shhh...let's stay quiet. They might provide more details about what happened to poor Mr. Williams," I suggested.

As the investigation and discussions continued, an ambulance arrived.

A team of doctors rushed to the crime scene, immediately diving into a flurry of tests and procedures over the past hour and a half.

"Guests, may I have your attention, please?" announced the burly cop, his authoritative voice silencing the room. Every eye turned toward him, captivated by his words.

"We regret to inform you that Mr. Henry Williams was the victim of an attempted murder. The assailant used an exceptionally sharp and precise instrument, not a typical knife, leaving a deep, visible cut on his upper neck. Our investigation suggests it was a sudden attack from behind, catching Mr. Williams off guard. The doctors have confirmed his critical condition; he's currently in a coma. We'll be transporting him to the hospital for further procedures. The next twenty-four hours are crucial. The wound, unlike typical cases of violence, is clean yet deep—an unusual and concerning characteristic."

"The reason we're disclosing this information at such an early stage is to emphasize that this investigation will be thorough and exhaustive. Even the slightest hint of suspicion will place you in a precarious position. I urge the perpetrator to step forward and make this process easier for everyone. Ultimately, you will be apprehended, so it's in your best interest to do so now. The consequences of your actions will remain the same. At the very least, spare the innocent from further suffering. We will be questioning all forty guests, as well as the waitstaff, assistants, security personnel, and Mr. Williams' family. If anyone has witnessed the murderer or suspects someone, please notify us immediately. The murderer is undoubtedly within this house. No one will leave this room without our permission. This will be a long and arduous night, and none of you are going anywhere!" the officer declared.

The detailed speech sent shivers down everyone's spine in the room, even Nats, known for her fearlessness. Her reaction was a stark contrast to her usual demeanor. As a chilling silence enveloped the room, Kyla suddenly exclaimed, "I know who the culprit, or should I say, culprits, are, Mr. Gary! Natasha, Shelly, and Kyle are the ones!"

My eyes widened almost to the point of popping out of their sockets and rolling onto the floor. Nats, now visibly shaken, retorted, "Are you out of your mind?"

"Absolutely not! I have concrete evidence," Kayla asserted.

"We are innocent, Mr. Gary," Kyle stated, his voice trembling inwardly.

"Please, go on, Kayla," said Officer Gary, setting aside Kyle's protest for the moment.

"Firstly, those three were always jealous of me for my success and my Dad's wealth that supported me in my career. Secondly, Natasha is skilled in sparring, which involves sharp weapons and could have possibly made the incision in the lethal spot. Thirdly, they disappeared from the dance floor for a very long time, about half an hour, if I'm not wrong. And lastly, Natasha was extremely scared after the announcement you made, and that's very unlike her. Kyle being afraid is normal, for he's the timidest of the lot, and Shelly, being the poker-faced one, also had a shocked expression on her face and appeared to have been scared as well. If this isn't conclusive evidence, I don't know what is," explained Kayla.

"Fair enough. Squad 805, escort the suspects to the precinct for a special interrogation," ordered Gary.

"Wait a minute, Squad 805! I just want to say that we were away from the dance floor because we were looking for Mrs. Peterson, who was not feeling well and went to use the washroom. It took us a long time to find her because the bathrooms are located far apart. Just because I know sparring doesn't mean that I know the perfect way of impaling someone! We use wooden wasters and not swords! I also want to clarify that we loved Mr. Williams, and we've known him since we were little. We would never do such a thing to him just because of his nasty daughter's conduct," said a daring Nats.

"Why should they be taken to the precinct? Why can't they be interrogated here?" Mom intercepted worriedly.

Squad 805 approached us without hesitation. "No, Officer, we aren't prepared for a 'special interrogation' because we didn't do anything *special*! How can you believe that imbecile?" Nats protested. Officer Gary paid no heed to Nats' objections, leaving us with no choice but to comply and follow them to the precinct. Little did I know what awaited us next.

As the officers closed in, Nats made a daring attempt to flee, triggering an adrenaline-fueled response that led Kyle and me to scatter in different directions. I immediately regretted my decision, knowing it would only raise more suspicion about the three of us. Out of the corner of my eye, I saw Nats pretend to accidentally spill wine on Kayla before making a run for it. I couldn't help but chuckle, but my laughter proved to be a grave mistake as the guards swiftly spotted and handcuffed me. I found myself caught instead of opting for the "special interrogation." I could only hope that Nats and Kyle had managed to escape.

Had he consented to the "special interrogation," it would have been preferable. However, he ended up getting caught instead.

Kayla shot Nats a glare that could kill, and I silently prayed that Nats and Kyle would elude capture. However, luck was not on our side that day. Within minutes, both were apprehended behind the food counter. Mom looked on helplessly, her spirit shattered, and I couldn't bear to see her in such anguish.

I attempted to console Mom, urging her not to despair further. "Mom, please don't shed tears over the actions of such ruthless cops! Instead of interrogating us like everyone else, they insisted on taking us to the precinct. They aren't worth your time or energy." I reassured her that, by the grace of God, we would return sooner than she anticipated. She was about to protest, but it was too late. The guards ushered us out of the Mayor's house, and I couldn't bring myself to look back.

Kyle and Nats didn't utter a word, their voices worn out from the endless yelling and pleading. The cops forced us into a waiting vehicle and quickly departed from the crime scene, taking custody of innocent college students. The smug satisfaction plastered across their faces sickened us.

"Let us out!" Nats' cry echoed through the confined space.

"There's no turning back now. If you had just agreed to the interrogation instead of running away, you might have stood a chance," Gary retorted, displaying an air of typical antagonism. He was resolute in his decision as he led us to our respective cells. The brutal cops ensured our isolation, placing Nats on the left, Kyle in the middle, and myself on the far right. "You have no evidence against us!" protested Kyle in confusion. "You fled when we approached to escort you for questioning," another cop reminded him before the sound of the lock clicked shut.

"You can't base everything on one person's account! She's just a vindictive and immature girl!" I attempted to reason, but Gary's stern and rugged appearance silenced me with a mere glance.

"Sir, it's enough to keep them quiet," remarked Gary's subordinate. I fought back tears, though the effort proved futile. Was this the taste of utter wretchedness? It was a sensation unknown to me until now, one I fervently hoped never to endure again.

"Can't you release us after the interrogation? You haven't even questioned us!" Kyle pleaded desperately.

"What's there to interrogate? You are clearly the murderers," the subordinate retorted.

"Just because we ran away?" Nats challenged.

"Obviously," he responded.

"Are you even a real cop? If you're accusing us of attempting to kill Mr. Williams, shouldn't you be asking us about how it happened, who was involved, and so on?" I questioned.

"Don't give them ideas, Shelly! They'll try to pin the murder on us," Nats cautioned.

"I'm not suggesting we are murderers; I'm just saying we are innocent and not afraid of interrogation. But they are not even questioning us. We ran away because we were scared, and we all know what a 'special interrogation' entails," I argued.

"These kids talk too much. We'll interrogate them tomorrow, and we'll make it extra special," replied Mr. Gary.

"Wait, if you question us today, we can avoid spending the night here, for God's sake!" I pleaded.

"This bunch is quite rebellious, aren't they?" Gary remarked. "Keep a close eye on their every move."

There was no way out now. I stared at the bars in front of us in disbelief.

CHAPTER 9
Headlines, here we come!

The headlines, undoubtedly, were the most astonishing part of the day. To our bewilderment, the cops weren't the least bit solemn. Kyle couldn't help but question, "Why are they smiling and, most of all, laughing? Are we in a dream?"

"Yes, Kai-Kai, dear! It is all a dream! We are in Shelly's house!" said a grumpy Nats. She paused and then yelled, "We are still imprisoned!"

"What happened, Squad 805? Why are you laughing like clowns?" I asked bluntly.

"Thanks to the three of you, we made it to the headlines!" replied one of the officers.

"Wait, what?" Kyle asked.

"Have a look!" he said, handing over a newspaper. My eyes darted from left to right as I scanned the headlines, rendering me momentarily speechless.

"Shell, what's up?" Nats inquired.

"Shell!" Kyle cried out to snap me from my trance. But still, I didn't say a word. Noticing my lack of response, the cop gently took the newspaper from my hands and passed it to Kyle and Nats. Their expressions mirrored my own, but Nats was livid. Not the usual fury, but a fiery anger that seemed to consume her entire being. "You'll pay for this, you jerks! Once I'm out, you'll be…" she threatened, making fists and pounding them into her open hand.

Even the cops appeared slightly rattled by Nats' statement, or perhaps I was merely hallucinating.

"How could you have the audacity to claim that everyone at the party accused us of attempting to kill the Mayor?" demanded Kyle, his tone stern.

"By the time we arrested the three of you, we were certain that everyone must have believed you were the culprits and would have accused you," Mr. Gary replied haughtily.

"Why did you have to mention the fact that I spilled wine on her? That's such a trivial matter!" yelled Nats, visibly incensed.

"Geez! Calm down! That isn't trivial. It suggests that you harbored a grudge against her, and that could be a motive for the Mayor's murder attempt," one of the cops chimed in.

"If I had a grudge against her, I would've probably killed her instead," Nats countered savagely.

"Make a note of her statement!" ordered Officer Gary.

"You have ruined our social lives! I could lose my job, my friends won't get theirs, and everyone will treat Mom with disrespect! Don't you get it? Revoke it! If you don't, we'll sue you once we're out of this desolate place!" I erupted.

My friends were astonished by my outburst, knowing I rarely lost my cool, regardless of the situation.

"That's a very twisted perspective, Gary" said a gruff yet familiar voice.

"But, Sir, we're just fulfilling our duty," replied a petrified Mr. Gary. The sudden shift in his tone amused me, and I couldn't help but laugh. He glared at me after acknowledging his senior.

"I know him," I whispered to my friends, a wave of surprise and a glimmer of hope spreading across my face as I recognized the cop I had met on the first day of my visit. Kyle's eyes gleamed with faith, but Nats remained skeptical about trusting any cop in New York.

"It's you!" I greeted him.

"Yes, dear. I didn't get your name that time," he replied.

"I'm Shelly. This is Kyle, and that's Natasha. What's your name, Officer?" I asked.

"I'm Officer Jones. I overheard your conversation, and in my estimation, you've arrested the wrong suspects, Gary," he replied.

"But Sir, we were just-" Mr. Gary began, but Mr. Jones cut him off with an expletive. "Your duty? My-***" he said. This was the first time I had ever witnessed an officer swear.

"The Mayor's daughter, Ms. Kayla, claimed that they were the murderers and provided undeniable facts. They attempted to escape when we decided to conduct a special interrogation for them," explained another officer.

"I don't delve into the facts unless I distrust the person. Kayla has been apprehended by the NYPD numerous times and was pardoned at the Mayor's behest. Release them!" Mr. Jones ordered. The cops had no choice but to comply with Mr. Jones's directive, and we were freed in an instant.

"Thank you, Sir," said Kyle, moving to hug him, but the Officer declined, finding it awkward.

"Sir, you should have come a day earlier! The news of our arrest has already been published," I added.

"I wasn't aware of it either. I was out of New York for an important matter and returned last night. I learned about the Mayor's attempted murder this morning and decided to investigate the crime scene. Upon my arrival, I was informed that the suspects had been apprehended, and I resolved to question them, only to find you, Shelly," explained Mr. Jones.

"But why did you release us on blind trust?" asked Nats.

"Because your friend here helped me identify a dangerous individual from afar," he replied, smiling at me, and I returned the smile.

"Natasha, are you Russian?" asked Mr. Jones, unintentionally making a gaffe with Nats.

"Officer Jones, I think you should change the subject as-" Kyle began.

"I'm not Russian. My name is Natasha, which is indeed a Russian name. My parents liked that name, so they named me that," Nats replied, managing to suppress her anger in front of the respected Officer.

"The ironic thing is that I was supposed to interrogate the three of you, but upon seeing you here, I was bewildered and decided to release you. However, I must still conduct a formal interrogation, so please answer my questions honestly," he said. He questioned us for about ten minutes with the standard queries and eventually declared us innocent as he couldn't find any incriminating evidence.

"Well, we're very grateful to you, Sir," Nats thanked him.

"So, what's happening at the Mayor's house? Before we were taken to the precinct, they mentioned that all the guests would be interrogated and would have to spend the night there. Are they all still there, and how's my Mom holding up?" I inquired.

"I don't know who your Mom is. As I said, I wasn't aware that I would find you here. Regarding the interrogation, yes, the guests had to remain there and were thoroughly questioned," Mr. Jones confirmed.

"So, did they find anyone suspicious and-?" Kyle started to ask, but Officer Jones interrupted, "I'll address all your concerns. But first, let me take you to your Mom's place. She must be worried sick," he suggested.

Mr. Jones was kind enough to drive us to Green Avenue all the way from the precinct. The turn of events had been entirely unpredictable, and I thanked God for sending us a knight in shining armor on the second day of our stay.

CHAPTER 10
More and more bummers

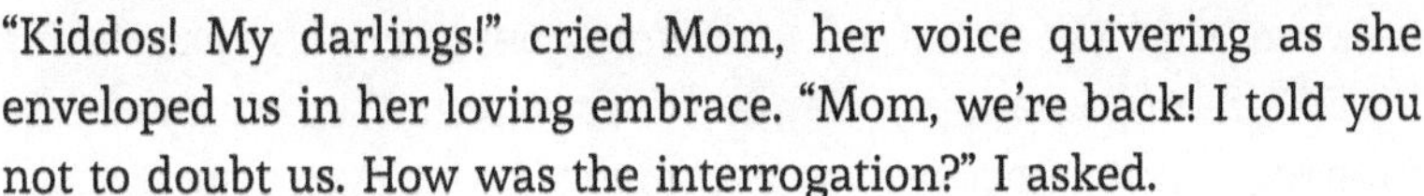

"Kiddos! My darlings!" cried Mom, her voice quivering as she enveloped us in her loving embrace. "Mom, we're back! I told you not to doubt us. How was the interrogation?" I asked.

"It was surprisingly good, but they were harsh with the staff," replied Mom.

"I'm starving," said Kyle, his stomach growling.

"I'm too drained to talk, Mrs. Peterson. Right after breakfast, I'll sleep," Nats added, her tone reflecting her exhaustion, which was unlike her.

"Yes, dear. Just come to the dining table. Who dropped you off here? You should've called me from the prison, Shelly," Mom insisted.

"Mom, this all happened very suddenly, just half an hour before. We reached here early because of less traffic. Mr. Jones, the Officer whom I helped on the day of my arrival in New York, dropped us here. He was also the one to release us," I explained.

"Well, God bless that man, for my kiddos are home safe and sound!" Mom said, her relief evident.

"Is Mr. Williams alive?" asked a frantic Nats.

"He is, but...I have this fear in my heart that he might not make it," Mom broke down. We comforted Mom by assuring her that Mr. Williams was a strong and resilient man and he would surely make it.

During the meal, I asked Mom a few questions about what happened right after we left. To our surprise, the cops' account was accurate, as Mom explained, "Yes, it's true. The foolish guests believed that the three of you were the criminals, except for the Welfare Committee. Despite your arrest, they initiated the interrogation to uncover any accomplices who may have assisted you in the attempted murder."

"Hey! We didn't attempt any murder!" I protested.

"I know, I'm just telling how the cops spoke. Now, where was I? Right, the interrogation. The forty guests were interrogated in alphabetical order and were asked a million questions. The interrogation began at roughly around 9:15PM and lasted until midnight for the guests, and until 1AM for the staff. I couldn't sleep because of Henry's condition and your arrest. The night couldn't get any worse for me," Mom recounted.

"Was Kayla interrogated, and what happened with Lydia?" Nats inquired.

"Even Kayla and Juliette were interrogated and were declared innocent. Lydia's interrogation was the longest, but not because she seemed culpable. It was because she wasn't giving straight answers and didn't want to narrate all the things she did at the party, like trying out a lot of food and all that," Mom chuckled.

"When can we go to the hospital to see Mr. Williams?" asked Kyle.

"Kyle, do you actually think they would let us go and meet him personally after we just came out of jail for being the suspects of an attempted murder?" I asked.

"I was trying my luck, you didn't have to put it that way," grumbled Kyle. "What happened, Nats?" asked Kyle as he realized that Nats was upset.

"Curse the cops and the entire NYPD, except Mr. Jones!" Nats swore.

"What happened, Natasha dear?" Mom inquired.

"All my friends have unfriended me and state that they regret befriending me in the first place. Even my closest friend did it in a second," Nats shared.

"This shows that they aren't your true friends, Nats. Don't worry, the three of us will face it together," Kyle consoled.

"What about Kyle and my parents, Mrs. Peterson? They must be disappointed in us for no fault of ours," Nats worriedly asked.

"I got that covered. I spoke to your parents just before you arrived and informed them about the series of events that took place," Mom assured.

"Thank you!" said Kyle and Nats.

"No, no, no! Just as I had expected. Apple fired me because of my arrest and wrote a disrespectful message to me," I wailed.

"At least we're out of prison, right?" Nats comforted me, and I hugged her.

After finishing breakfast, Nats, Kyle, and I dropped off to sleep, undisturbed for three hours until the doorbell disrupted my peaceful slumber.

I cursed at the doorbell as it shattered the peace of my deep sleep, which was a stark contrast to my friends who lay still, lost in the soothing embrace of slumber. I begrudgingly got up from my bed and shuffled after my Mom. "Who is it?" I asked her.

"It's the cops," Mom replied with a weary tone, another bummer!

"Kyle, Nats, wake up! The cops are at our doorstep," I urgently roused my slumbering friends. "They woke up with a jerk and combed their hair to look presentable. A police officer greeted us. "Good afternoon, Ma'am. I apologize for disturbing you during lunchtime, but can we interrogate Natasha, Kyle, and Shelly as part of the protocol for the Mayor's attempted murder case?

"No, you may not, as they have already been interrogated by Officer Jones," Mom retorted.

"Ma'am, we are aware of that, but we must interrogate them in the same manner as the other guests," the cop informed.

"They have been treated differently from the other guests with a 'special interrogation' and by being arrested! They are innocent, and you still want to interrogate them!" Mom's temper flared.

"We sincerely apologize for the misconduct of Officer Gary and his squad. However, we kindly request permission to conduct an interrogation, as we believe it may yield valuable leads in our ongoing investigation of the criminal," explained the cop.

"I'll let this pass, but this will be the last time any cop from the

NYPD messes with my daughter and her friends!" Mom sternly warned.

"Yes, ma'am, it won't take long," he replied, and instructed the three of us to come one by one. The procedure took half an hour, and they politely thanked us for our cooperation.

"Quick it seems!" smirked Nats.

"We're clear! Hooray! They won't disturb us again!" Kyle exclaimed with relief.

"Yeah, good thing we mentioned the man who gave us the masks as a witness," I added.

"Fortunately, the man mentioned it himself during his interrogation," Nats explained.

The doorbell rang again, but this time, it was a different squad of cops. "Good afternoon, Ma'am. We have come to interrogate-" she said when Mom replied, "The three of them have already been interrogated."

"Oh, I see. Thank you for not making this investigation any harder for us. If you've heard, our detective squad is tied up with a top-secret, confidential case," she explained.

"Aren't there any other detectives in other precincts in New York?" Nats inquired.

"Detectives are scarce in number, and they are all engaged in the case I mentioned. The ones we consult are the Sherlock Holmes of New York," she replied.

"The cops have decided to step in and take this case as their responsibility," stated the second cop.

"There aren't any detectives? Seriously! I thought NYC would have loads of them!" Kyle exclaimed after the cops left.

"The criminals have to pay for the terrible time we had in prison and for destroying our reputations!" Nats declared.

"I couldn't agree more! But since there aren't any detectives around, we'll have to step into those shoes ourselves," I said.

"What do you mean?" Kyle asked.

"We'll take it forward from here. We'll be the detectives!" Nats replied with determination.

CHAPTER 11
Examining the tragedy

"It's all settled then," confirmed Kyle.

"Not so fast. Knowing the NYPD, they will not let anyone meddle with this case, especially," said Mom.

"We'll unmeddle it for them," replied Kyle.

"I doubt that's a word, but offering a fresh perspective on the crime could be beneficial, Mrs. Peterson," Nats reasoned.

"I'm just concerned that if you guys can't apprehend the culprit and they escape, you'll be publicly scapegoated," explained Mom.

"We are willing to take that risk," I said with a mischievous grin.

With Mom relenting to our sound reasoning, we successfully obtained permission to investigate the crime scene. We left the house with a sense of pride and triumph.

"Where are we going, Shell?" asked Kyle.

"Straight to the scene of the crime, detectives!" I declared, embracing the role of a true sleuth.

"How will we bypass the cops?" Nats inquired.

"I'm not sure. We'll have to think on our feet," I replied.

"So, you're saying we have no plan?" Kyle cross-questioned.

"You could interpret it that way, although it does sound somewhat pessimistic," I admitted.

In just four and a half days (considering I arrived in New York at night), everything had changed. From a casual tour around New York to reconnecting with my ex-best friend, getting invited to her party, witnessing her father's attempted murder, being imprisoned, and now embarking on our own investigation- it had transformed from a poorly planned tour into complete and chaotic mayhem. For those who found my book hard to follow, this is the summary.

As we arrived at the Mayor's house, we instinctively made our way to the gate, only to be halted by the familiar set of security guards.

"What's your business here?" one of them inquired suspiciously.

"Weren't you supposed to be behind bars?" added the other guard.

"The most frustrating part is that you all bought into the idea that we were the perpetrators, when in fact we were innocent! Kayla has a tendency to manipulate situations. Don't trust her blindly. She might just fire you for her father's misfortune due to perceived security lapses," I remarked, trying to sway their judgment.

"That would be terrible, wouldn't it?" Nats interjected.

"Hold on! We'll need to verify with the cops whether you should be allowed in," the first guard responded promptly. They hurried off to the gate, where Mr. Jones was also present.

"What brings you here?" Mr. Jones questioned, eyeing us with curiosity.

"We've volunteered to assist as detectives. We heard there's a shortage of detectives at the moment and thought we could lend a hand. The more, the merrier," I explained.

"Your help isn't necessary. We have the situation under control, and as they say, too many cooks spoil the broth," Officer Jones replied firmly.

"Sir, we could be valuable assets in catching the culprit. We're resourceful and clever," Nats persisted, trying to convince him.

"Being clever isn't the only requirement for being a detective. It takes keen observation skills to spot subtle clues and hints in a mystery," he countered.

"I did spot the culprit last time," I interjected.

"That is true, but she was right in front. I mean, she was detectable by your eyes, but clues and hints in a mystery aren't that explicit," he explained.

"Since you're not open to listening, here's a proposition. Let us investigate the crime scene today. If we can't offer any valuable insights by tomorrow, we'll never bother you again. But if we do, you'll give us a chance to prove our innocence by allowing us to find the real murderer," Kyle proposed, surprising us with his boldness. His proposition was a risky one, but if we wanted something, we must be willing to take a leap of faith.

Officer Jones deliberated for a moment, exchanging glances with his colleagues, before finally agreeing to the deal, despite the skepticism of the others. They escorted us inside the Mayor's house.

Memories of our last encounter with Mr. Williams flooded my mind, evoking a bittersweet smile. As we were ushered upstairs to meet with the other officers and Juliette, her sharp tone cut through the air.

"Why have you brought them here?" she demanded, her gaze fixed on us with suspicion.

"Ma'am, they're not the ones responsible. They've been thoroughly interrogated, and one of your waiters confirmed they were nowhere near the staircase," Mr. Jones explained, trying to reassure her.

"Still, I can't trust them, Officer," she replied.

"Juliette, please trust us. We're here to assist. We care deeply for Mr.Williams and are committed to aiding the authorities in nabbing the criminal. If we don't make any headway today, we won't impose on you further," I reassured.

Though Juliette wasn't entirely convinced, I refrained from passing judgment. Eventually, she relented to our pleas, granting us permission to enter the Mayor's room.

A pungent stench permeated the air, indicating the presence of old blood. We were astonished to see a motionless dummy corpse seated in the antique armchair.

"How did this—" I began to question, but another officer swiftly interjected, "We chose not to disturb the scene, preserving it as is.

If you'd like, you can wear these masks," he offered, handing each of us a set.

"Now is your opportunity to provide your insights," Mr. Jones urged.

"First, let's examine Mr. Williams; then, we'll assess his position and his surroundings; and finally, we'll identify any potential clues," instructed Nats.

"Before we proceed, could you please provide us with any information about fingerprints or other potential clues you may have noticed?" Kyle inquired.

"Prior to your arrival, we repositioned the dummy corpse in its original seated position. As for fingerprints, we didn't find any on the Mayor's clothing," replied the officer with a badge on his collar.

"Here are your gloves," said Mr. Jones and handed each of us a pair.

"Well, it looks like it's up to us to begin the investigation. Will you lend us a hand?" I asked the officers.

"You're on your own today. If you can't make any headway, you won't be permitted to return tomorrow," Mr. Jones asserted.

"Do you have a picture of Mr. Willaims' wound?" I asked.

"Here you go," said Officer Jones, handing over the photo.

"Great!" exclaimed Nats as she approached Mr. Williams. She examined the wound on his shoulder, which was exactly as Mr. Gary had described. Adjacent to Mr. Williams' left shoulder was a hollow injury, narrow but deep. Although the bloodstains had been removed, the wound still bore a faint scarlet tinge. It was evident that the Mayor had bled profusely, but the criminal had managed to partially clean the wound before escaping.

You might find it intriguing that a stab in the shoulder could incapacitate the Mayor, as typically, fatal stabbings target well-known vital spots like the chest. However, the reason he fell into a coma was due to the major arteries running through the shoulder. Stabbing elsewhere would have likely hit fat or muscle. In fact, the shoulder houses the most vulnerable set of arteries," Nats explained.

"We are aware of the assault on the Mayor, but tell us, why did the perpetrator target the neck?" asked the cop with the badge.

"Sure, Sir. There are two potential scenarios regarding the Mayor's death. Initially, a stab to the neck seemed unusual. Consequently, we have considered two possibilities. First, the assailant may not have intended to kill the Mayor but accidentally inflicted a fatal injury with a knife. Second, it's plausible that the criminal deliberately targeted the Mayor's shoulder to create the impression of an unintentional accident," I suggested.

"That seems unlikely, Shelly," replied Mr. Jones.

Why, Sir? Perhaps an assistant of the Mayor approached to serve refreshments and accidentally dropped the plate, causing the knife to impale his shoulder. Or maybe someone came to present an ancestral sword or knife to the Mayor. There are countless scenarios to consider, and we shouldn't rush to conclusions with the current evidence," I explained.

"I hadn't considered that, but it seems improbable," replied another cop.

"We have an idea of what might have transpired," declared Kyle. Juliette's eyes shone with hope. "Mr. Williams was stabbed from behind but did not immediately fall into a coma. He saw the murderer and engaged in conversation until his last moments. We can assume that he attempted to shout for help but wasn't audible because of the lively party, or perhaps he refrained because he knew he couldn't escape his death. Either way, he was stabbed, and blood oozed from his shoulder rapidly. He attempted to stall the attacker by engaging them in conversation while trying to stop his shoulder from bleeding excessively," stated Nats.

You're correct, Natasha, but there's one additional detail to consider. I'll explain, Officer. Upon examining the Mayor's shoulder again, I noticed two incisions. The first one is the prominent wound just below his left shoulder, while the second one is situated on his pectoral girdle and is less severe than the first. It appears that while Mr. Williams was attempting to prevent blood loss, the assailant made sure to incapacitate him further with the final blow to his shoulder," I added.

"That sounds convincing, but how can you be certain that these events unfolded in this manner?" questioned another cop.

"We can't say for certain, but you requested our input, and this is our interpretation, Sir," replied Kyle.

"Fair enough, you're hired. You'll be working with us until the case is closed," declared Mr. Jones. Nats, Kyle, and I felt triumphant and elated.

"Officer Jones, were the doctors able to determine when he slipped into a coma?" I inquired.

"The doctors analyzed changes in his brain activity and vital signs to estimate when the coma occurred. It happened between 7 and 7:15-ish," he replied.

"That was during the Masquerade ball," remarked Nats.

"Exactly an hour before it was discovered! Impressive," said Kyle.

"The criminal must have had accomplices; otherwise, it would have been impossible to execute such an elaborate plan. This suggests an inside job," I stated.

"Ms. Clover, was the room exactly like this when you entered to call for Mr. Williams?" asked Kyle.

"Yes, Kyle. The windows were closed, but the door was unlocked. All his pens were neatly arranged, and his documents were stacked in a tidy pile," Juliette described.

"That seems highly unlikely," replied Kyle.

"I have to agree with him. During a murder attempt, things tend to get disrupted," supported Mr. Jones.

"Did you notice anything unusual when you entered the room?" Nats inquired.

"I had this strange sensation in my stomach, like the air was heavy with the scent of fresh blood. At the time, though, I didn't realize he had been stabbed, as he was seated perfectly in his armchair. That was all," replied Juliette.

"Is there anything else?" Nats pressed, leaning towards Ms. Clover with curiosity.

"There's this thing I just remembered. Along with the stench, I could smell traces of something burning," she added.

"Burning? There isn't a fireplace in this room," said Nats.

"I'm not sure why the culprit would burn something, but I distinctly smelled it upon entering," she replied.

"Thank you, Ms. Clover, for your valuable time. If you could excuse us to discuss matters regarding the murder attempt?" I asked politely.

"Certainly,"she said politely and closed the door after her. Her behavior had changed since the incident.

"Officers, we have to re-conduct the interrogation with the staff," I insisted.

"But why should we? We already interviewed all of them thoroughly. We were rigorous and detained anyone suspicious for further questioning, and they all passed," objected one of the officers.

"There are several loopholes in this case. Despite the security check, the criminal managed to possess a weapon. Even if they didn't carry it, they must have gained access to it within the house, which wouldn't have been possible without an accomplice on the inside!" I emphasized calmly, without raising my voice.

"Couldn't you spot anyone climbing the stairs a little before 7 in the CCTV footage?" asked Nats cleverly.

"That's an issue I discovered today. I was mad at them for not informing me earlier. The ground floor CCTV cameras stopped working around five," replied Officer Jones.

"That's terrible! Shelly's right; it seems like an inside job. Have you contacted the person in charge of that?" inquired Kyle.

"Surprisingly, the four people vanished during the party. There are four individuals in charge of each wing of the ground floor of the Mayor's house, as it is colossal," explained Officer Jones.

"Could you track them down?" asked Nats.

"We tried, but they were gone. It's as if they were never here," replied another cop.

"What about the first-floor cameras? The criminal might have been spotted there since they weren't switched off," I pointed out.

"There aren't any cameras on the other floors. The Mayor was against anything that infringed upon the privacy of his family members. He believed he had no enemies and was even opposed to installing CCTV cameras on the ground floor. However, after much persuasion, he finally agreed to it," clarified Officer Jones.

"That explains a lot," I said disappointedly.

"Speaking of CCTV cameras, aren't there any in this room for Mr. Williams' protection?" inquired Kyle.

"Why would there be? Like I said, they would violate the Mayor's privacy," explained the second cop.

"That means the murderer knew a lot about Mr. Williams and was also aware that there aren't any CCTV cameras in here," contemplated Nats.

"We asked Ms. Clover where the Mayor had his meetings with the Welfare team and she said he attended those downstairs. So, it must be one of the staff members," added the third cop.

"But why did you want Ms. Clover to leave?" Officer Jones asked me.

"That's because she may be one of the accomplices," I replied.

"Why do you think so?" asked the third cop.

"When Natasha asked her about what she observed, she didn't state much, but when she asked Juliette a second time, she gave more information. Another thought that continued to nag at me was her apparent lack of regular check-ins with her fiancé, the Mayor, throughout the party. I know he told everyone not to disturb him, but she didn't even go upstairs once, which is fishy," I explained.

"That makes me doubt her a lot, Sir," said a cop to Mr. Jones.

"Re-interrogating the entire staff would take a lot of time, and we need to close this in three days," said Officer Jones.

"Can you please provide a count of the staff?" requested Kyle.

"There were four security guards, eight waiters, four people in charge of the CCTV cameras, and one personal secretary of the Mayor. Of those, sixteen remain since the ground floor CCTV camera lady left," replied another cop.

"We'll interrogate all of them but will divide the work. The three of us will interrogate the eight waiters, while the cops and Officer Jones can interview the security guards and the CCTV authorized personnel. Lastly, all of us will interview the personal assistant because that's critical," I instructed.

"The four cameramen disappeared, remember? We'll interview the guards. But we should finish the interviews by tomorrow and then re-interrogate a few of the guests if necessary," agreed Officer Jones.

"Would you like refreshments?" asked a cop.

"It would be nice," said Kyle hesitantly. "Rosa, six glasses of orange juice, please?" he requested.

"Yes, Sir, coming right up," replied a cheerful voice.

"She's also one of the waiters, and don't inform them about the interrogation," instructed Officer Jones.

Rosa arrived within five minutes carrying a tray with six glasses of freshly made orange juice, which she then served to us. We thanked Rosa for the beverages and complimented the delightful flavor of the orange juice. Nats and I had left our sling bags on the floor and I was too lazy to fetch them back, so I requested Rosa to hand over the blue sling bag to me. She went towards the two bags and accidentally gave the purple sling bag, which was Nats's.

"Rosa, the blue one," I reminded her.

"Yeah, right. So sorry, Ma'am. I don't know why I gave you the purple one. I wasn't paying attention and gave you the first one I saw, Ma'am," she apologized.

"It's all right. We all make mistakes occasionally. Could you please pass the purple one?" I requested, and this time, she came with the right one. I thanked her and she responded with a pleasant smile before leaving the room a little while later.

"She's one of the kindest waiters I've met," remarked Kyle.

"Yes, she is. She joined a year ago, as far as I know," replied one cop.

"If you don't mind, Officers, can we please conduct the interrogation of the Mayor's personal secretary?" I inquired.

"Why not?" said Officer Jones and called for him.

CHAPTER 12
The Interrogation of Wayne Smith

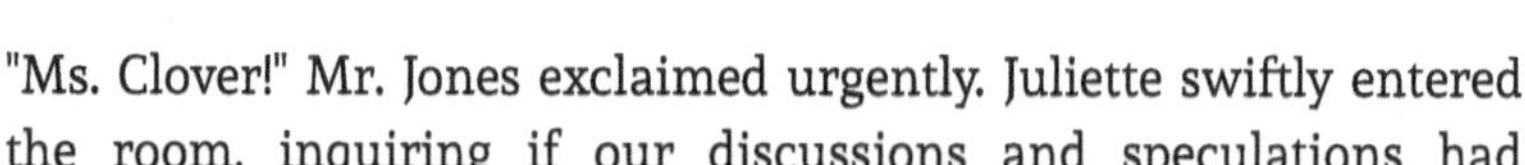

"Ms. Clover!" Mr. Jones exclaimed urgently. Juliette swiftly entered the room, inquiring if our discussions and speculations had concluded.

"Ma'am, we are done with our discussions. We wish to interrogate Mr. Williams' personal secretary," informed one of the cops.

"I understand. I'll inform him, though it may be unnecessary as he's known for his loyalty," replied Juliette before leaving the room.

"We cannot trust anyone, especially the personal secretary. He is the closest to Mr. Williams and knows his daily routine," stated Nats.

"You're correct, but Ms. Clover vouched for his loyalty to Mr. Williams. I don't foresee an issue," said Kyle.

We can't be certain, Kyle. Those closest are often involved," I added.

"Sirs, did you call for me?" asked a gentle voice as the personal secretary entered the room. He was a dark-skinned, tall, and lanky man, with a fancy coat and suit.

"Yes, we did. Are you the Mayor's personal secretary? If so, we must interrogate you," declared Mr. Jones.

"Again? Is something wrong? I stated I've asserted my innocence, and Mr. Gary declared me innocent," said the flustered secretary.

"There's nothing wrong, Wayne. We are redoing interrogations for all staff. You aren't an exception," explained the first cop.

"I think we should move to another room for the interrogation, Officer," I suggested.

"Agreed. Wayne, could you show us to a spare room?" requested Mr. Jones.

"Sure, Sir. Follow me," Wayne directed, leading us through a long, narrow corridor with rich red carpeting reminiscent of medieval palaces. Wayne opened the door to a spacious, serene room adorned with intricate floral designs on white walls, and courteously held it open for us, ensuring everyone entered before him.

"Is this your office?" inquired Kyle.

"Yes, Sir, it is," Wayne confirmed.

"Have a seat, Wayne," instructed the third cop.

"After you, Sirs," Wayne gestured, arranging chairs for the officers and offering to fetch more, when I said, "It's alright, Wayne. We'll stand for now."

"Are you sure, Ma'am?" he asked.

"This won't take much time," assured Nats. Wayne finally took a seat, looking apprehensive as the interrogation loomed ahead.

"Officer Jones, would you like to begin?" prompted Kyle.

"I'll start if that's what you prefer. Feel free to ask any questions," he replied.

"Sure, Officer," replied Nats.

"First off," began Officer Jones, as the first cop interjected, "Have a glass of water, Wayne. Don't be nervous. We aren't here to arrest you or anything of the sort, and we won't jump to conclusions."

Wayne nodded, taking a deep breath and sipping from the glass. "I'm ready now, Officer," he said.

"Excellent. To begin, what are your duties as the Mayor's personal secretary?" Officer Jones inquired.

"I handle all documents, serve meals, and attend to his various needs," Wayne answered.

"Did he give you any specific instructions before the party?" Officer Jones continued.

"Yes, just one. He didn't want anyone entering his room and instructed me not to do so either. However, I did check on him every hour," Wayne replied.

"When was your last check-in?" Kyle inquired.

"I'm not entirely sure, Sir. It was a little before seven," Wayne replied.

"Just before the stabbing," Nats remarked.

"I swear to God I didn't stab him. I never would. I've been with him for four years now and would never betray his trust," Wayne insisted.

"We're not accusing you, Wayne, though others might suspect since you were the last to see Mr. Williams before he slipped into a coma. Did you happen to see anyone near the Mayor's room? Like someone approaching the door or something?" I asked.

"Not a soul, Ma'am. I made sure no one disturbed him," Wayne replied.

"I see. There's something peculiar for sure. The murderer was not seen on the first floor and managed to appear in the Mayor's room. There's only one possible explanation," I replied.

"Which is?" asked the third cop.

"Someone entered through the window. I know it was closed when Ms. Clover entered, but the criminal likely closed it afterward. Someone who wasn't invited to the party may have managed to bypass the security," I suggested.

"If that's the case, this criminal of ours has had many accomplices in this house, which is why we're re-interrogating the staff. For now, let's focus on who the culprit might be," Officer Jones instructed.

"Did you hear any sounds after you left?" Officer Jones inquired.

"Come to think of it, I did, Sir, while descending the stairs. It sounded like something toppling, but I assumed it was just part of the party," Wayne added.

"It must be the window then. Officers, please interrogate the security guards thoroughly, especially considering one let an old lady with poison slip away," Nats explained.

"Wait, why wasn't this reported earlier?" asked the first cop.

"It was a misunderstanding. The 'poison' turned out to be asthma medication, but it's still worth investigating," Kyle clarified.

"May I leave, Sirs and Ma'ams, if my interrogation is done?" asked Wayne.

"Not yet, Wayne. A few more questions. Why did you check on the Mayor before seven?" asked Officer Jones.

"To remind him about Kayla's cake cutting. He seemed preoccupied, so I thought it best to give him a gentle reminder," Wayne explained.

"How well do you know Juliette?" Officer Jones asked.

"Not very well, but she's not a stranger to me," Wayne replied.

"Do you also serve her?" I asked.

Actually, I don't. Ms. Clover has her own personal secretary. I simply assist her with occasional small favors," Wayne clarified.

"We're done with your interrogation for now," Officer Jones informed.

"Before I take my leave, may I pose a question? Weren't the three of you arrested? I hope you don't mind," Wayne inquired.

"Not at all. Yes, we were, but thanks to Mr. Jones, we were released," Kyle replied.

"One more thing. Do you know of any staff member capable of betraying the Mayor?" Nats asked.

"There is one person who comes to mind: Aaron, one of the waiters. He has a history of disregarding the Mayor's instructions and has been involved in arguments with him. While I can't say for certain, it's certainly worth considering," Wayne responded thoughtfully.

"Thank you for your input, Wayne. You may leave whenever you wish to ," I said. Wayne bowed in gratitude and quietly exited the room.

CHAPTER 13
Aaron's interrogation

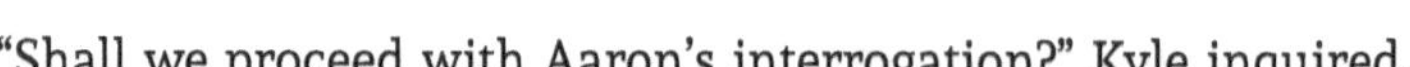

"Shall we proceed with Aaron's interrogation?" Kyle inquired.

"Only Natasha, Kyle, and I will conduct it since he's one of the waiters. The officers can question the guards and the CCTV cameramen," I suggested.

"Sounds good! Just make sure to keep us informed if Aaron's interrogation doesn't proceed according to plan," Officer Jones instructed.

"What exactly do you mean by 'doesn't go as planned'?" Nats asked.

"If his profile matches that of the murderer, or if he creates a ruckus during the interrogation, tries to escape or anything of that sort," answered Officer Jones.

"Gotcha!" Kyle replied. "We'll interrogate that suspicious security guard you mentioned. By the way, can you describe what he looks like?" asked the third cop.

"Just remember, he's the taller of the two security guards. He has a long face and tends to wear a perpetual smile," Nats described.

"Wow, you seem to have observed quite a bit about him!" I teased.

"He seemed suspicious, so I paid attention. I don't normally stare at people," Nats justified.

"We need to get going," said Officer Jones, leading the other two cops out of the room.

"Ms. Clover, could you come here for a moment, please?" I requested.

Juliette hurried into the room like an eager cat.

"Shelly, did you call me?" she inquired.

"Yes, Ma'am, I did. Can you please fetch Aaron for his interrogation?" I asked.

"Aaron? That name doesn't ring a bell," she replied.

"He's the rude waiter," Kyle explained.

"Oh, that guy! I didn't know his name was Aaron. Well, now I do. I'll go look for him," she replied.

"Wait, Ma'am!" I cried out. Juliette turned and looked at me hesitantly.

"Did you meet Mr. Williams in the hospital?" I asked.

"They wouldn't let me, dear. They forbade Kayla as well and stated that we weren't allowed to meet him until he is conscious," she replied with a face that evoked sorrow and helplessness.

"I see, carry on then," I replied and she left at once.

"That's weird...They didn't even let Mr. Williams' immediate family visit him," remarked Nats.

"It's not surprising after what happened at the party," suggested Kyle.

"Shelly, are you ready with the questions?" Kyle asked.

"I'll come up with them on the spot. After all, it depends on Aaron," I replied.

After a minute or two, Juliette entered the room with a towering man. "I found Aaron," Juliette announced.

"Thank you, Ms. Clover," I expressed my gratitude, and she left the room.

Instead of describing Aaron as "tall," I used "towering." You'll understand why once you see him for yourself. Aaron was a tall yet hefty waiter with a protruding belly and pale skin. His eyes were sunken in their sockets, and his nose was broad with a huge zit on its tip. He was bald but had a long mane. To be honest, Aaron's appearance was intimidating.

"Good afternoon, Aaron. Please have a seat," I greeted him. Aaron didn't have the courtesy to offer a greeting and simply sat down.

"We have summoned you for an interrogation regarding the attack on Mr. Williams," Nats informed him. When these words left Nats' lips, Aaron's face displayed disbelief and astonishment. He swiftlyy rose from the armchair and made his way to the door. Kyle rushed towards the door, blocking his way, and said, "Please stay, Sir. You can leave once we're done with the interrogation."

"I'm innocent and don't need an interrogation! You're wasting both our time," he growled, making himself appear culpable.

"This won't take much time, I promise," I reassured him.

"If it takes more than five minutes, I'm out of here!" he declared.

"Relax, Aaron! It will be quicker than five minutes," I assured him. This time, he remained seated.

"Were you deeply saddened by the tragic incident?" Nats questioned.

"I wasn't. Life and death are natural. Everyone has to die at some point, and besides, he's still alive," he answered. We were taken aback by his response. The Mayor was fighting for his life at that moment. He nearly died and might not even make it!

"Mr. Williams was stabbed, Aaron. It was an attempted murder," I replied.

He didn't utter a word for a moment before asking, "What's the next question?"

"Do you assert that you were loyal to the Mayor?" Nats inquired.

"What do you think?" Aaron cross-questioned. "We're not certain, Sir. These are the standard questions we've prepared for the staff," I covered cleverly.

"I was loyal to him. I may not have been a bootlicker like Wayne but I swear that I was loyal," he affirmed.

"If that's true, then why didn't you always obey him?" Nats asked.

"I had my reasons too. Sometimes, I didn't agree with his

instructions, and other times, I simply wasn't in the mood," replied Aaron casually.

"Not in the mood? Is that another way of saying you openly opposed him?" questioned Nats.

"Did Wayne rat me out? It sounds like he talked behind my back to you," stated Aaron.

"You figured it out, Aaron," I intercepted to save time.

"What did he say exactly? Because I have a secret of his," blurted Aaron.

"Say what?" exclaimed Kyle in astonishment.

"Hold on, Aaron. Wayne didn't divulge much. When we pressed him to identify a possible betrayer of the Mayor, he mentioned your name," I responded.

"Shelly!" exclaimed Nats angrily, realizing I had revealed our conversation with Wayne.

"It's better to cut to the chase, Nats. What is this secret?" I asked.

Aaron smirked with contempt and looked at me. "At half past seven, I was serving refreshments to the guests in the south wing when I looked up at the staircase and caught a glimpse of Wayne" he explained.

"Wayne? At half past seven? That was after..." gasped Nats.

"Was it? I wasn't aware of that. Anyway, when I glanced at him, coincidentally, our eyes met. He appeared distressed for some reason, but I assumed it was because he saw me. You know, he was always apprehensive around me, so I attributed his unease to that. However, I had a gut feeling that he was concealing something. When I decided to head upstairs to investigate, he promptly went in the opposite direction toward his room, as if to avoid me."

"No way! Wayne came out of the room at half past seven!" cried Kyle.

"Go on! What did you pause for?" asked Nats as she didn't want to be kept in the dark. She never really liked to be left in suspense during cliff-hangers.

"Nothing much after that. He knew I saw him and that's the reason why he gave my name when you asked for a person who could betray Mr. Henry. He is guilty as hell," he said with an evil glint in his eyes.

"Then, why didn't you tell Mr. Gary about him?" I asked.

"Mr. Gary? Who is that?" he asked quizzically.

"One of the police officers in the NYPD. He had conducted the interrogation for the guests as well," reminded Nats.

"Oh, yes! I wasn't in the mood to rat him out. Why am I being interrogated again?" he asked in anger.

"Sir, that's because Wayne told that you could be culpable," answered Kyle.

"He did it on purpose and I hope you realize that. You have to re-reinterrogate him," said Aaron and broke into a guffaw.

"How come the CCTV cameras didn't spot him at half past seven!"

wondered Nats.

"You have to deal with those people, not with me," answered Aaron.

"How did you remember the exact time when you saw Wayne coming out of the Mayor's room?" I asked.

"I looked at my watch to see the time, and that's when I casually looked up at the staircase to see Wayne," he replied.

"Interesting, we must inform Officer Jones! It's urgent! Before Wayne escapes!" cried Kyle.

"We will, don't worry," I assured.

"Time's up! I am leaving now," said Aaron as he rose from the armchair.

"Thank you for your input," I said, but Aaron had already closed the door.

"We didn't get to ask him the other questions! There were many more," yelled Nats.

"That doesn't matter now. We've identified the murderer. It's Wayne, for sure! No one was seen climbing up the stairs because Wayne was already on the first floor, so he wasn't caught on camera," I explained.

"Shelly's right, we need to apprehend Wayne immediately!" said Kyle in agreement.

"We shouldn't inform Officer Jones about this yet," I stated.

"Are you crazy?" asked Nats.

"No, I'm not. They are interrogating the guards now, and if we accuse Wayne, the guards might escape in the commotion. There's a possibility that one of the guards is an accomplice," I explained.

"But we've identified the murderer, the right one!" emphasized Nats.

"Eureka!" cried Kyle in an ecstatic tone.

"What is it now?" asked Nats, sounding grumpy.

"Simple, we'll just request Wayne's presence during the interrogation of the other eight waiters. That way, we'll ensure he doesn't slip away without him realizing it," replied Kyle.

"That's a little tricky. What if Wayne asks us why he should be present?" I questioned.

"We'll tell him we need his opinion on the matter since he must know the staff well, and we can instruct him to keep an eye on them after the interrogation too," answered Kyle.

"That sounds good. Should I call him?" asked Nats eagerly.

"Go ahead," I said.

"Wayne! Could you please come here?" she requested.

"This will be interesting," said Kyle with a mischievous grin.

CHAPTER 14
Mystery Woman

"Wayne!" cried Nats when he failed to appear promptly.

"Oh, I'm so sorry, Sir and Ma'am. I was assisting Ms. Clover," he responded, a reply that only heightened my suspicions.

"No worries, Wayne. We called you to bring in Rosa, the waitress, for questioning," I explained.

"I see, I'll bring her right away," he said. I quickly gave last-minute instructions to Nats and Kyle on how to conduct themselves while interviewing Rosa, emphasizing the need to not make Wayne suspicious.

"That's a lot of words, but I'll try to follow a few of them," Nats cheekily replied.

"No, you won't!" I retorted with the deadliest stare ever. Wayne returned with Rosa within a few minutes, preventing me from providing further instructions. Doubts lingered - were we doing the right thing? Should we have called 911 or Officer Jones?

"Did you call me, Ma'am?" asked Rosa in the most courteous manner.

"Yes, Rosa, have a seat," I said with a smile. She smiled back like an angel and took her seat. As I observed her, I noticed Wayne discreetly heading towards the door, but Nats intervened, "Wayne, can you please stay back? You were the Mayor's personal secretary and I'm sure you know all the staff members. You can verify whether what Ms. Rosa says is accurate and ask questions if needed. We aren't accusing you, Rosa, but we're taking precautions."

"Ah, that's fine," Rosa responded casually, displaying no signs of being perturbed or emotional.

Though reassuring, we pressed on with the interrogation. "Have a seat, Wayne. Let's begin, shall we?" said Kyle. Rosa nodded, and Kyle initiated, "What were you doing a little before seven?"

"Uhm, I was serving food in the south wing," she answered. "She was in charge of serving the south wing guests but I'm not sure whether she was there at that time because I had gone to check on the Mayor. However, I did see her around half-past six, so I guess she was there," confirmed Wayne.

"Thank you very much," replied Kyle.

"Hey, Rosa," Nats inquired, "assuming you didn't witness anything unusual while serving in the south wing, did you happen to notice anyone heading up the stairs?"

Rosa sought clarification, "Which stairs, Ma'am? Oh, the staircase to the Mayor's office?"

"Yes, that's the one. My bad for not specifying. I meant the Mayor's office staircase, not Juliette's," clarified Nats.

"Juliette doesn't live here," Rosa responded, and that's when I began to realize she might not be the sharpest one around. In fact, calling her a 'dunce' might be an understatement.

"You didn't need to answer that, Rosa, but did you happen to see anyone?" I asked, trying not to let my frustration show.

"No one went upstairs. I did see Wayne go upstairs at half-past six, just as he mentioned, but nobody else after that. He was running errands on the first floor," Rosa replied.

"Any idea who might have planned this against Mr. Williams? Perhaps someone among the house staff?" I probed.

"I can't say for certain. I've only been here for four months, so my judgment might not be the most reliable," she replied.

"But do you have any suspicions? Nats asked impatiently.

"No names, Ma'am. Everyone seems fine to me," answered Rosa.

Aaron was right. It appeared Wayne mentioned his name out of fear. Wayne had painted Aaron as argumentative and disobedient, and he seemed to fit Wayne's description as he was laidback and didn't cooperate with us. However, that was because we were kids, according to him.

"Are you loyal to Mr. Williams?" Kyle asked.

"What do you mean by loyal, Sir? I'm just his waiter and if you're asking about whether I would betray him by leaving his service ever, then, no, I wouldn't do that," Rosa replied.

Nats nudged Rosa, showing her disapproval of the irrelevant question.

"So, Rosa, how many waiters served in each wing since there are eight of you? I assume there are two per wing?" Nats cleverly asked.

"Yes, Ma'am, two waiters for each wing," Rosa confirmed.

"Who was the waiter who served along with you?" asked Nats.

"Aaron was my partner," stated Rosa.

"Oh, yes, we interrogated him," I chimed in, and Kyle requested, "But please, don't inform the other waiters that they would be interrogated next."

"Sure. Any more questions?" Rosa asked.

"Actually, there is something I want to ask," Wayne jumped in. "Did you see anyone mysterious or suspicious on the ground floor after seven? Someone who didn't quite fit in?"

The color from Rosa's face faded, and her expression changed. She seemed taken aback. "Thanks for reminding me, Wayne. I told them about her but they couldn't do anything about it," she answered.

"Told who about whom?" asked a confused Kyle.

"During the first interrogation itself, I informed Officer Gary about a mysterious person, but he came back to me saying he interrogated all the guests, but none of them remembers seeing anyone like that," explained Rosa.

"Not even Aaron?" Nats asked.

"He wasn't near the bathroom, so he didn't see her," Rosa clarified.

"What do you mean by that?" I asked, pressing for more details.

"I saw her near the south wing's bathroom as she walked close to me. After that, I went to serve beverages to one of the guests, so I couldn't see where she went," explained Rosa.

"Did any of the guests see her?" I asked.

"I'm sure a few would have, but they must have forgotten about it or wouldn't have been able to describe her features to Mr. Gary, I guess," she added.

"Can you describe her?" asked Nats.

"She was tall and wore a beautiful purple gown with a feathery black cloak covering her entire body, showing very little of her. Her dress camouflaged with the surroundings, and her hair was jet black and straight," she described.

"What did you find weird about her?" asked Nats.

"Her mask was what intrigued me. It wasn't one of the masks we had given to the guests. You see, we had chosen eight colors for the guests: orange, green, pink, red, yellow, purple, blue, and black. But the lady's mask was white, and that's when I understood that she brought her own mask and had known that there was a masquerade ball in the end; but that was supposed to be a surprise for all. Officer Gary asked whether anyone had seen the lady that matched my description, but there was no response. Most of the guests didn't pay attention to their surroundings," answered Rosa.

"Can you describe her more? Her dress or her physical appearance?" asked Kyle.

"Well, she had worn long sleeves and black high heels. She was white, and she walked in a rather odd manner, and when she bumped into me, she didn't even say sorry," added Rosa.

"She seems to be the one, Rosa. Thanks for your time and valuable inputs," I said, and Rosa got up from her seat and closed the door silently.

"We have a huge clue now! Let's analyze the situation and catch that lady. Wayne, did you see anyone like her?" I asked, trying my luck.

"Unfortunately, no, Ma'am. I was on the first floor at that time. I came downstairs at around 7:15," he replied.

"Did you go upstairs again?" asked Nats.

A bead of sweat rolled from his nose down to his chin, or maybe I had imagined that. He then answered after a while, denying the allegation. Just when I was about to trap Wayne, Officer Jones barged into the room hastily, clutching the hand of a boy around our age.

"What's the matter, Mr. Jones? Did you catch the murderer?" asked Nats.

The boy froze in shock and cried, "You brought me here to arrest me? I'm not the murderer! Believe me, Officer!" cried the boy, and was trying to escape when Officer Jones said, "You got it all wrong! I brought him here to show a video he had taken during the party," explained Mr. Jones.

The boy heaved a sigh of relief and sat on a chair. "Why don't you introduce yourself?" asked Kyle.

"Sup guys! Vivek here, Kayla's second BFF, life adviser slash fashion designer," said Vivek.

"You design her clothes? How old are you?" asked Nats eagerly.

"Yes, I do, and I'm nineteen years old, but consider me a twenty-year-old cause I'm going to be one in a month," he said jovially.

I was shocked to see such a young fashion designer, and I'm not gonna lie, Kayla's clothes were amazing, including the gamer girl outfit.

"Woah! You're so talented!" said Nats exultantly on finding someone like her.

"Enough with the intros, Vivek. Show them your video," ordered Mr. Jones.

"Yeah, about that; I was creating a vlog for Insta, so I shot a video of Kayla's party when I noticed a mysterious lady in the background of the video," explained Vivek.

"Do you mean a lady wearing a white mask along with a purple outfit with a black feathery cloak all over her body?" asked Nats.

"How did you-?" asked Officer Jones, with bulging eyes. Kyle explained everything to Officer Jones and Vivek.

"Rosa turned out to be useful! Have a look at it for more clues" urged Mr. Jones. Vivek passed his phone to us, to look at the video.

The clip commenced with Vivek narrating animatedly about the details of Kayla's party. Shortly after, he moved to his left and approached the bathroom area where Rosa accidentally bumped into the Mysterious Woman.

"Can you please pause the video?" I requested. He nodded and asked me whether he had paused it at the exact time. I said, "Can you please go back a little? About ten seconds behind?" He paused the video, and that's when I noticed a part of Wayne's body climbing down the stairs.

"What time was it when you shot this part of the video?" I asked.

"I'm not too sure," answered Vivek, trying his best to recollect his memories. He suddenly broke into a wide smile and said, "How could I have been so stupid? The time when the video was taken is visible next to it. Let me check Gallery," he said and took the phone back. "I started shooting this video at 7:39, and the scene of the video which you asked for was shot after 2 min 28 sec. That means, the time was 7:41 or 7:42," he replied.

"That was quite clever, Vivek," praised Nats.

"Thanks a ton, Vivek! Officer Jones, we have our criminal or maybe an accomplice," announced Nats.

"Nats! I told you to be patient!" I cried.

"Well, I believe in the saying - Better late than never. Officer Jones, the culprit is none other than the loyal Wayne!" declared Nats.

Wayne looked as though he were struck by lightning. He didn't even have time to react as Officer Jones swiftly handcuffed him and escorted him out of the room.

"What's going on?" asked Vivek, bewildered.

"Nothing much, we found someone who seems to be involved, but we weren't supposed to disclose it yet. Unfortunately, Natasha couldn't contain herself," explained Kyle.

"I want to come too!" insisted Vivek.

"Sorry, buddy, next time," said Kyle as he left the room.

"Thanks again, Vivek! Let's stay in touch," I said gratefully, and he smiled back, remaining in the room.

I pondered how someone as nice and humble as Vivek ended up being one of Kayla's best friends. Perhaps she befriended him solely for his design skills. Regardless, justice for her father was paramount, and I was determined to deliver it. Hang in there, Mr. Williams, we're on the brink of apprehending the culprit.

CHAPTER 15

Only the Truth

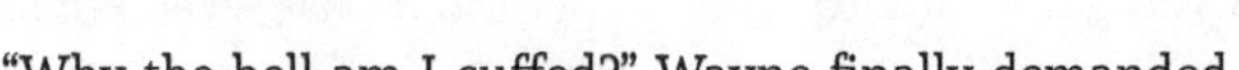

"Why the hell am I cuffed?" Wayne finally demanded.

"I'm not entirely sure myself, but I followed Natasha's instructions, and they wouldn't ask me to cuff someone for no reason," Officer Jones replied.

"Well, what's the reason, Natasha?" Wayne asked angrily.

"Many reasons, in fact, and I can't count them on my fingers because there are so many," Nats replied.

"I'll tell you those reasons," I interjected. "Wayne was the last person to meet Mr. Williams when he was conscious, just as he said, and admitted that quite casually, right Wayne?" I asked, locking eyes with him.

"Yes, I did, but that doesn't mean-" cried Wayne, but I swiftly cut in, "Hold on, there's more to it. You never mentioned that you came out of the Mayor's room at about half-past seven, which was quite some time after his attempted murder. You even denied it when I casually brought that up during Rosa's interview."

"I- i- obviously denied it 'cause I was freakin' not there!" Wayne protested.

"Are you sure about that? Your good friend Aaron informed us that he spotted you coming out of the Mayor's room at that time! Do you mean to say that Aaron is blind or saw your identical twin and got confused?" Nats added with a hint of sarcasm.

Wayne was silent and didn't even look up. "He also told us that you went into another room when he spotted you, which means you were guilty," Kyle chimed in.

"Oh my god! You got it all wrong! It was not half-past seven when he saw me! It was seven or maybe a little before seven. He got confused, and I went into another room as I had a few errands to do, not because I'm guilty," Wayne explained.

Nats's face turned red, and I could hear her curse Wayne under her breath. "Wayne, you moron!" she exclaimed.

"Natasha, chill. He can't escape because we have evidence against him. If you look at the video properly, at 2 minutes and 28 seconds when the time was 7:41 or 7:42, you can see Wayne coming down the stairs. This shows that he had gone upstairs to the Mayor's room! The only person who knew the Mayor's house so well and also knew that there aren't any CCTV cameras on the first floor was Wayne! He denied going upstairs after seven, and here's a glimpse of him coming down the stairs," I explained.

Officer Jones' face was aflame. He glared at Wayne and dragged him across the room towards a chair, tying him up. Wayne was in a horrendous state. He broke down, and his eyes gave way to a waterfall of tears. He cried to such an extent that I wondered whether the room would be submerged if he cried any longer.

"Please don't arrest me! You got it all wrong once again! I'm not the murderer; let me explain!" Wayne pleaded, sobbing and coughing. Being the kind of person he is, Kyle handed him a bunch of tissue papers.

"Why the heck are you handing him tissue papers!? Are you siding with a criminal?" Natasha asked in an accusatory tone.

"I don't know; it felt like the right thing to do," Kyle replied.

"I don't deserve it, man. But thanks. I'll tell you everything, but please believe me, I'm not the murderer," Wayne said, his voice choked with emotion.

"You better tell the truth! Only the truth will be accepted!" yelled Officer Jones, his patience wearing thin.

"Before you say anything, can you please reveal the identity of that Mysterious Woman?" I asked, trying to steer the conversation back to the critical point.

"I don't know her! Like I said, I am not related to the crime in any way!" Wayne cried, his voice trembling with desperation.

"Go on! Tell the truth! I won't hold back anymore!" Officer Jones demanded in an unwavering tone.

"Fine! I'll tell you about it. Yes, I went to Mr. Williams' room a second time at about 7:25-ish, and-and," Wayne hesitated. "That was after his attempted murder! You tried to kill him!" Natasha cried.

"No, no! When I went to his room, I found Mr. Williams unconscious! At first, I thought he was sleeping on his armchair, but after a while, I concluded that he was dead! I know he's alive now, but in that moment, I genuinely believed he had passed away," Wayne explained, his voice tinged with regret.

"What did you do then?" I inquired, trying to piece together the events.

"I stood there for a moment in shock and then proceeded with my plan," Wayne replied.

"What plan? Can you please give us the details without us asking you all the time!" demanded Nats.

"Sorry, I won't do it again. I went into Mr. Williams' room to st-st-stea-stea-steal his watch," Wayne finally opened up.

"You what?" asked Kyle.

"My family isn't doing well. My uncle was injured in a car accident, and we didn't have enough money. I asked Mr. Williams for a salary hike, but he objected. I was going to tell him about my uncle, but he was extremely busy the last few days. At last, I decided to take things into my own hands and planned to steal one of his expensive watches and sell it for a fortune. When I went into his room, I tried to engage him in conversation and subtly move towards his watch collection. But when I started speaking to him, he wasn't responding, and that's when I realized something was wrong. I went towards him and noticed a deep wound on his neck. Thankfully, I didn't touch him, so my fingerprints weren't on him. I didn't know what to do and left the room hastily. I decided not to tell anyone about his death as it would make me look suspicious. Imagine if I called 911 after spotting him unconscious, who would they suspect? Me, obviously!" he explained.

"Did you steal the watch or not?" asked Officer Jones.

"No, I didn't. I was petrified, so I fled the crime scene," replied Wayne.

"Interesting, but why should we believe you? You must have been the killer," I stated.

"As you can see in the video, I don't have a knife or any sharp object in my hand," Wayne answered.

"Maybe you kept it in another room," I suggested.

"Ma'am, I went into the other room out of fear of being spotted by Aaron! I didn't do anything! I didn't even wear gloves to hide my fingerprints, and that's what murderers do!" justified Wayne.

"I believe him," declared Kyle.

"We can't let him loose yet! All the clues lead to him! He knew the house very well, the Mayor very well, his schedule very well, and the locations of the CCTV cameras. He wants us to believe that he casually went into his room to steal a watch and instead found him unconscious and didn't do anything about it and just left? I can't think of any other person who's capable of killing Mr. Williams," replied Officer Jones.

"You're right about all the facts, but there is one thing that favors him, and that is, why would he kill the Mayor?. He had no enmity for him and was pleased to be of service to him. He even swore today that he never betrayed him," I added, trying to reason out.

"How does that matter? He thought he killed him and left instantly, and nothing was heard because of the loud music," explained Officer Jones, dismissing my argument.

"Sir, may I please remind you that the loud music began playing from seven to seven twenty or seven fifteen. I went after that, and by that time, he was already stabbed. I didn't spend much time in his room and was back in five minutes! The doctor declared that he was killed between seven ten and seven twenty, but I went into his room after seven twenty!" explained Wayne in a desperate tone.

"How do we know that you went after seven twenty and not before that! You told us that you went to check on the Mayor at seven or a little before that, but you never mentioned leaving his room after that. You must have stayed there till seven thirty! You were spotted by Aaron at seven thirty! You assumed the Mayor was dead and opened the door at seven thirty! Even a toddler can spot the criminal in such a scenario!" yelled Officer Jones in fury.

"But I came out at seven to make sure the party was going on according to the plan! You can ask Aaron! He saw me downstairs at seven!" stated Wayne.

"I'll look for him," said Nats and left the room.

"Did you call me?" asked Aaron within a minute.

"Yes, we did. We just had one question for you. Did you see Wayne downstairs at seven or a little before that?" I asked.

"Yes, I did," answered Aaron and said, "What's the matter about? Is Wayne caught? I saw him at seven thirty as well, and have you cuffed him because of that?" asked Aaron.

"It's because of that, and we're grateful for your info. Thanks to you, we got to know that Wayne was up to something, but he isn't the criminal," I stated.

Wayne's face broke into a smile, and he was glowing. "Thank you, Aaron, for confirming that you saw me at seven," said Wayne.

"I just told the truth, but what were you doing at half-past seven?" asked Aaron.

"I'll tell you later," said Wayne in embarrassment.

"You can leave now, Aaron, but Wayne, you'll still be cuffed and tied here as a safety precaution," declared Officer Jones in a firm yet empathetic voice.

"Thank you, Officer, for not arresting me! I shall be grateful to you!" said Wayne.

"Officer Jones, let's leave this room and have a discussion elsewhere," I recommended, eager to regroup and reassess the situation.

"Sounds good, we're leaving you here," he said and closed the door.

"So, is the murderer the Mystery Woman?" asked Kyle.

"Most probably, let's have a look at that video once again, and after that, we can return the phone to Vivek," suggested Officer Jones.

We scrutinized the smallest of details in the video, and I was shocked by with what I noticed. "Can you please pause the video?" I requested.

"What's the matter? Did you spot anything uncanny?" asked Kyle.

"Look at the lady's arms! She's wearing black gloves," I stated.

"Maybe it was just a part of her party attire?" said Kyle.

"That is possible, but I noticed a red dot on her gloves," replied Officer Jones.

"Let me zoom it in," I said, eager to examine the evidence more closely.

"No, there isn't a speck," replied Nats.

"Oh ok, I must have seen something else. She isn't the criminal either," said Officer Jones, disappointed by the lack of conclusive evidence.

"Don't worry Officer Jones, we'll find the criminal," I assured, determined to pursue every lead until justice was served.

"I hope so, I must get going now. I found one of the guards suspicious and left him there with the other cops. Call me if you find some hints," he said and left us to continue our investigation.

"Back to square one, I guess," commented Nats and rolled her eyes in frustration.

CHAPTER 16
More and more Allegations

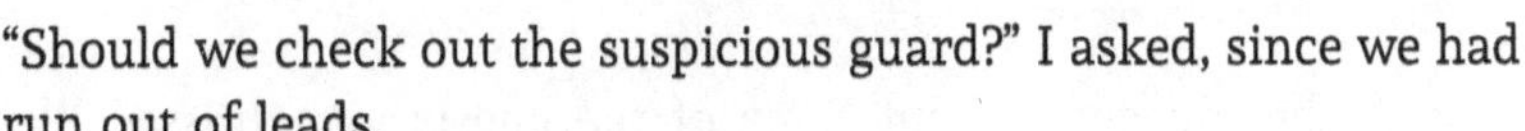

"Should we check out the suspicious guard?" I asked, since we had run out of leads.

"That would be sensible," agreed Kyle.

"I'll hang out with Vivek then," said Nats.

"No, you're coming with us," I insisted and took her with me.

We approached the entrance of the Mayor's house and discovered Mr. Jones and the other two cops interrogating the guard whom Nats had found suspicious.

"It wasn't poison, Sir! I swear! It was a syrup," the guard justified nervously.

"If it was just syrup, then why did your partner suspect it to be poison?" Officer Jones questioned skeptically.

"He is a newly appointed guard, Sir, so he was taking more precautions and was trying to be impeccable in his security check," the suspicious guard explained, attempting to defend himself.

"Is that true?" Officer Jones asked the other security guard.

"He is correct, Sir. I was just trying to do my best to impress the Mayor, but we couldn't spot the murderer among them," replied the other guard.

"Did either of you spot anyone wearing this outfit or carrying any of these belongings during the security check?" I inquired, displaying a picture of the Mystery Woman. The guards scanned the image intently, examining it as if they possessed X-ray vision. After a moment, they both shook their heads in disappointment.

"She is the murderer then! None of the guests was dressed like this, and this proves that one of them was disguised as this lady and impaled Mr. Williams!" Nats exclaimed.

"Why would anyone change their outfit in the middle of the party for no reason?" wondered Officer Jones.

"To look different for the masquerade ball, I guess," suggested Kyle.

"Even if she isn't the murderer, she'll definitely be an accomplice and will give us leads," concluded Officer Jones.

"Sir, you can do a house check for all the guests to check their belongings. You'll surely find one of these things she's wearing like the purple gown or the cloak," the new guard suggested.

"That's perfect! Thanks!" cried Kyle in excitement.

"We can do the house checks after interrogating the entire staff. Shelly, if you don't mind, we'll have to check your house too," informed Officer Jones.

"Not a problem!" I assured.

"We'll get going then. Six more waiters to go," declared Nats.

"What about Wayne?" asked Kyle.

"What about him? He lied straight to an officer's face. It's punishment for him," replied Officer Jones.

"Let's do the interrogations fast! Officer Jones and his team have to interrogate only two more guards," I instructed.

"Do it asap! We'll go ahead with the house checks after lunch. We'll have lunch at one and will start the house checks by two," he replied.

"Sounds good! We'll get going," said Nats.

We made a detour to Mr. Williams' house. "How come Kayla isn't here?" asked Kyle.

"It seems that Ms. Clover sent her to a friend's place to enable us to interrogate others here more freely," I suggested.

"I'm starving! Let's wrap up the interrogations quickly. But how can we? There are six more waiters!" stated Nats.

"A group interrogation seems sensible. We can all question the six waiters," suggested Kyle.

"But won't that make it easier for them? They could lie and agree to each other's lies," I replied, expressing concern.

"How about we each interview two waiters? We'll be done with six in half the time!" squealed Nats.

"That sounds perfect! We'll go with that plan," I agreed, and Kyle nodded in approval.

"Do you want any drinks?" asked Rosa. "I'll have a strawberry milkshake," said Nats. "That was quick," I remarked. Rosa turned to us, asking politely," And what about you two?"

"I don't want anything," replied Kyle. "Neither do I," I added, and Rosa left to fulfill the order.

"Hey, Rosa, before you leave, could you please call in the other six waiters for their interrogation? We don't know their names, so can you randomly send in a waiter?" I requested.

"Yes, Ma'am, I will. One at a time, right?" asked Rosa.

"Yes. Also, the three of us will interrogate two waiters each in separate rooms to save time. We must conduct house checks to find the belongings of that woman you met. Can we get three rooms?" I asked.

"Yes, Ma'am, there are many rooms here. I'll send one waiter to your room, his room, and her room," she replied. "Can you give us rooms that are far apart? We don't want the waiters to hear each other's questions," instructed Nats.

"Sure, come this way," directed Rosa. The corridor was long and empty. "You can take the room on the extreme right, Sir can take the one on the extreme left, and Ma'am can take the room in front of us," she stated.

"Don't call us Sir and Ma'am, Rosa. You must be our age," I said. "I'm twenty-three," replied Rosa. "A little older than us, then," responded Nats.

"Thank you for your help, Rosa," we said collectively. "No problem, I'll send them in, but not at the same time," she replied before leaving.

After forty minutes, the three of us finished interrogating the six waiters. "How was it?" I asked.

"Very bland. I mean, there was nothing interesting, cheeky, naughty, or suspicious. The two waiters I interrogated were grandpas! They couldn't have laid a finger on him and were nowhere near the south wing," explained Nats.

"Mine were innocent too," added Kyle. "Well, same here! We're done with it then! Let's grab lunch," I insisted.

"Should we go home? This place is deserted and huge; I'm getting creeped out," said Nats.

"Haha, we'll stay here and have lunch. Mom is at Jade's place for lunch. She apologized a lot to me for not being there to cook lunch," I explained.

"I don't blame her; she must be pretty shocked. Her friends must be comforting her," replied Kyle. "I hope she gets back to her regular self soon. Rosa!" called Nats.

"Yes, did you call me?" she asked in her customary courteous voice.

"If you don't mind, can you please inform the Mayor's chef that we're staying here for lunch? We didn't even ask Ms. Juliette for permission, but we're starving, and..."I started, but Rosa interrupted, "No worries! The three of you are working tirelessly to catch the criminal for Mr. Williams' sake! He insisted that the three of you have dinner here a few days ago as well. This will be a favor for him from my side."

"You're the best, Rosa!" said Kyle, giving her a hug. "Thank you so much," I replied, and so did Nats.

"It will take forty-five minutes for lunch to be cooked," informed Rosa.

"Will you have lunch as well?" I asked out of concern for her slender figure.

"Yes, I will, along with the other waiters in a shared room. But thanks for asking," she replied.

"Shelly, what is this game you sent to me?" asked Nats on checking Messenger for the first time today.

"It's a color game. You have to say the name of the color in which the word is written, not the word," I explained briefly.

"I'm very good at this," declared Kyle overconfidently. "Hold up, you don't know one thing! The words are names of other colors!" I declared.

"That's tough, but let me give it a shot!" said Kyle, snatching the phone from Nats's hand and diving into the challenge of saying the names of the colors instead of the color in which the words were written.

"Gah! This is tricky! You try it, Nats!" he said, handing the phone back to her.

She read, "Yellow, bl- no, brown, orange, purple, black, yellow, red."

"Wrong! The last one isn't red; it's pink! You read the word instead of the color," corrected Kyle.

"I got the last word only wrong! Damn it!" said Nats, and Kyle and I burst into laughter.

Rosa approached us and informed that lunch was ready. "Hey, Rosa, why don't you try this game out?" I suggested, explaining the rules to her.

"Okay, then! Let's go," she said and began reading. She made several mistakes on her first fewr attempts but almost got it right on the fourth one.

"I have an idea! Let Rosa try to read all the colors, and at the end, we'll point out her mistakes." suggested Nats. We all agreed, and Rosa read, "Yellow, brown, orange, blue, black, yellow, pink. Did I get it right?"

"Nu-uh! Not quite! You said blue instead of purple. It is purple in color," Nats pointed out.

"Wait, let me double-check! No, it is blue! Oh wait, my bad, it is purple indeed! "she admitted.

"Lunch's ready!" announced a voice from the first floor. "Coming! I must go," Rosa said, returning shortly with a mouthwatering pizza on a large platter. "You guys are in luck! Today, he made Italian, which is my favorite and must be yours too," she informed with a smile.

"It is! Thanks!" we exclaimed, eagerly digging into the pizza.

"I'll go now to have my lunch," Rosa said, excusing herself.

"Please, go on!" I said as she left.

We finished our lunch in half an hour and were ready to leave.

"Rosa, we're leaving," informed Nats and urged us to leave quickly. "Guys, we must hurry; it's half past two! We should help Officer Jones in the house checks! The more people we have, the better our chances of observation," she explained.

"Let's go! But we don't know where Officer Jones is! Shelly, do you have his number?" asked Kyle.

"Nope, I don't, sorry!" I replied.

"Let's just call 911," suggested Nats with a grin.

"No! no! Not that, Nats. Let's just go home. If he comes to look for us, Rosa will inform him that we left, and he might come to our place," I replied unsurely.

"I don't think that will work. Let's inform the guards!" replied Kyle and spoke to the guards for a while before coming to us. "We can go now!" he said, and we left the Mayor's house.

"Today was tiring. Is it fine if I sleep in the afternoon?" asked Nats, attempting to evade the investigation.

"No, we'll have to work on the case with Officer Jones. We're really close, and I can feel that! What if Officer Jones finds the Mystery Woman's outfit? Let's not lose hope," urged Kyle.

"I don't have a good feeling about Sassy Granny for a long time now. Can we interrogate her now that we have nothing else to do?" asked Nats.

"No, leave her alone! We'll go home and wait for Officer Jones," I replied.

"You guys are dumb! She is the murderer! She seemed to be fashionable as well," justified Nats. Kyle and I ignored her and walked all the way home. Upon ringing the bell, we were shocked to see Mom in handcuffs along with Officer Jones!

"What's going on!?" I asked indignantly, surprising Officer Jones, who had never seen me lose my cool before.

"He came to our house for a house check and found this fluffy black cloak in my closet! This isn't even mine, Officer! You must believe me, ask them! Ask them if they came across this in my closet! They went through it before the party!" requested Mom.

"Officer, this must be a mistake. We did go through her closet for gowns, and Shelly and I never came across this! Even if we didn't find it, she must have bought the same cloak, I guess. But she insisted that she had never seen this in her flat, so she must be telling the truth. Please Officer, don't arrest her! Mrs. Peterson isn't that kind of a person!" pleaded Nats.

"I can't do anything! I'll take her to the precinct, and you can meet me there," he replied gingerly and left.

"Mrs. Peterson! Don't worry; we'll get you out!" assured Kyle, but I doubted Mom heard that. This was enough! We had to find the criminal now! Clearly, the murderer placed her disguise in Mom's flat.

"Guys, I realized something! The murderer has hidden her disguise in innocent people's flats. The cloak was found in our home, which means the other garments and the white mask will be found in others' flats," I explained.

"You're right! We have to inform Officer Jones! Let's take a cab to the precinct! I'm sure other people like Mrs. Peterson will be present there!" agreed Kyle.

"But I didn't expect that from Officer Jones," I said in disappointment.

"He was just doing his job as the NYPD head," replied Nats.

"But I didn't expect him to be like Mr. Gary! He cuffed Mom without any proof!" I stated.

"There was proof. The Mystery woman's cloak was the proof, but we know that someone wanted Mrs. Peterson to take the fall," explained Kyle.

We got into the cab and left for the precinct. Thankfully, we reached in fifteen minutes! I got out of the cab and ran towards the station. Officer Jones was seen along with Courtney, Trina, and Mom! All the members of the Welfare Committee except Jade were there.

"You've got to be kidding me!" said Nats after seeing the other two people in the precinct.

"Officer Jones, why are they here too?" I asked as curiosity got the better of me.

"The white mask and the exact pair of black gloves was found in Trina's flat, and the purple gown was in Courtney's flat," replied Officer Jones without looking at me.

"I never ever owned such an expensive gown! I went through my closet this afternoon to decide what to wear. We went to Jade's for lunch, and when I come home, the cops are at my door requesting for a quick house check, and kaboom, an exquisite gown which I never found in my closet is lying over there, and the next thing I know, I'm cuffed and am at the police station," explained Courtney in detail.

"That's exactly what happened to me and Grace," justified Trina.

"Officer, can't you see they are innocent? It's implausible for them to coordinate with friends and plan how to lie to the cops about the garment, especially when they had no prior knowledge of the impending house check," Kyle reasoned.

"It's entirely possible, Kyle. Perhaps their mutual friend, Jade Mc, who heads the Welfare Committee, casually informed them, or maybe Shelly inadvertently mentioned it to her Mom," Officer Jones replied.

"Did you know Shelly?" Mom inquired.

"Yes, I did," Mom.

Addressing Officer Jones, I replied, "I didn't get the opportunity to inform her about this amidst the interrogations. Mom's inquiry should reassure you."

"But isn't it odd that they couldn't spot the garment? Surely, they would have sifted through the closet while putting their clothes back and wear home clothes, yet none of them noticed it," remarked Officer Jones.

"Officer, the cloak was tucked beneath my scarves, and why would I take a look at scarves during summer?" Mom countered.

"Fair point. And what about you, Trina?" Officer Jones turned to her.

"Sir, I didn't rummage through the sock section of my closet during the check. Since you were conducting a thorough inspection, you must have come across the white mask and the black lace gloves there," Trina explained.

"Interesting, but like Grace's situation. And you, Courtney?" inquired Officer Jones.

"My circumstances are entirely different. As you can see, I'm still dressed in my outdoor attire, not my home clothes. After lunch at Jade's place, I visited an old friend of mine. When I returned home, the police were there, and I was taken aback. When I got to know about the house check, I was cool and composed, knowing I had nothing to hide. However, when they found the dress in my closet, they cuffed me, and I was clueless as to why they did that. When they showed me the picture of a woman wearing the same outfit, I was shocked. That dress isn't even mine, but someone clearly wanted to frame me," Courtney explained.

"I believe the three of you, but as a precaution, I must detain you overnight. Before proceeding, I have a question: Who could have known that Grace owned many scarves, that Courtney had plans elsewhere after lunch, and had access to your flats?" Officer Jones' inquiry left Mom, Courtney, and Trina stunned. What an excellent question!

"I'm about to reveal that person's name," Trina informed Mom and Courtney.

"Please, don't. It couldn't be her. She wouldn't do such a thing," Mom pleaded.

"I agree with Grace. Accusing her might put her in a difficult position," Courtney added.

"Who else could it possibly be, Officer? You know it, I know it, and they know it too. It is none other than Jade McCallen," Nats declared, and everyone stared at her in horror.

CHAPTER 17
The Burnt Letter

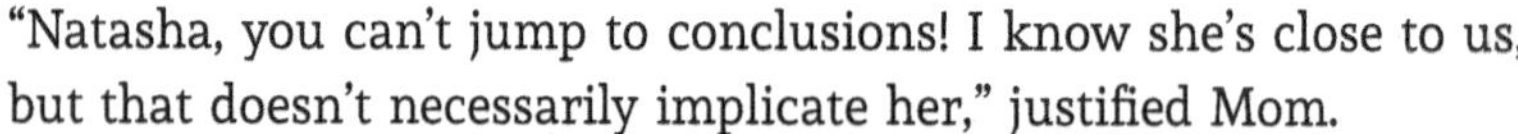

"Natasha, you can't jump to conclusions! I know she's close to us, but that doesn't necessarily implicate her," justified Mom.

"True, but why are the belongings of that woman found in the flats of all the Welfare Committee members except Jade? It's suspicious that it's absent only in her flat," questioned Nats.

"She has a point," Trina concurred.

"But what motive would Jade have?" Courtney pondered.

"Perhaps someone else planted the evidence to incriminate Jade deliberately," Kyle suggested.

"Kyle has a point. We can't rush into interrogating Jade without concrete evidence against her," reasoned Officer Jones.

"So, what's our next move? There doesn't seem to be anyone else who could have done it, unless the keys were hidden in obvious places like under the doormat," Nats stated.

"Trina might have left her keys in a spot outside her flat, but it wouldn't have been an obvious one," Mom added. "Besides, we all have each other's keys," Trina informed.

"Then perhaps we should pay a visit to Jade's house," Nats suggested eagerly.

"Let's hold off for now. We can gather more information, like who holds grievances against the Welfare Committee members. Someone may have orchestrated this to cast suspicion on Jade," Officer Jones proposed.

"But how would they have obtained the keys?" I queried.

"That's a bit more complex, but I've heard of methods to pick locks using a pin," Kyle chimed in.

"Not a bad theory, Kyle. So, what's our plan, Officer?" Nats pressed impatiently.

"We'll return to Mr. Williams' house and review the CCTV footage before five," Officer Jones decided.

"We'll get going, Mom, Trina, and Courtney. Don't worry, Officer Jones knows you're innocent," I reassured. None of them responded, likely too upset or worried about Jade.

Leaving the station, we headed to Mr. Williams' house in the police vehicle. But as we stepped out of the van, a thought struck me. "Officer Jones, shouldn't we address the clue Ms. Clover mentioned?"

"What clue?" Kyle interjected. "The burning smell," I clarified.

"Yes, I think we should re-examine his room and question Wayne about it. If he mentions it, he's likely innocent; if not, we may have our suspect," I suggested.

"Speaking of Wayne, what if one of the staff members unties him from the chair and lets him escape?" asked Nats.

"That's a valid concern, but I've got it covered. I stationed two cops to guard him just before we left," he replied.

"Let's not waste any time, then!" urged Kyle, and we hurried to the crime scene.

"But what significance does the burning smell hold, other than implicating Wayne?" inquired Nats.

"The presence of the burning smell suggests that the culprit may have set something ablaze. It could be a crucial clue," explained Officer Jones.

"After this, we're going to Jade's flat, promise?" clarified Nats.

"Yes, we will! Let's get started now!" exclaimed Officer Jones. We quickly ascended the stairs to reach the first floor. Wayne remained composed in his chair, surprisingly unfazed by the situation. "I don't mind spending the day here," he remarked, initiating conversation.

"We'll release you once we determine your innocence or guilt," declared Nats.

"Did you notice anything when you entered the room?" I asked.

"Yes, as I told you, I heard a faint thud after leaving Mr. Williams' room, but I didn't go back in," replied Wayne.

"No, that was when you entered his room the first time, aka the time before the murder. I'm referring to your second visit," I clarified.

"Ah, the second time. Let me think," replied Wayne.

"We don't have all day, Wayne. We have other tasks to attend to, so please cooperate," Officer Jones stated sternly.

"I totally understand, Officer, but I must put in effort to remember the minutest of details. I'll do it in a minute," he replied and remained silent for a while. A million thoughts were racing in my head whether he would confess or not. At last, he said, "I remember something, though I'm not sure if it's significant. When I entered the second time, I noticed a faint burning smell. It wasn't very strong, but it was definitely there."

"In that case, he's innocent, Officer. You can release him," said Kyle.

"I'm only untying him from the chair! He'll remain handcuffed," replied Officer Jones.

"As a matter of fact, that is an important clue. Mr. Williams wouldn't have lit his fireplace during the party, so the only plausible explanation is that the culprit burned something as a hint or clue," I deduced.

"What should we do about it then?" asked Kyle.

"Let's search this room thoroughly. Every nook and corner should be visited. We might uncover something valuable," I suggested.

"Let's don our detective hats then!" remarked Nats, promptly initiating the search for any clues on the floor. I headed towards the windows to inspect for any signs of burn marks, while Officer Jones, Wayne, and Kyle scoured Mr. Williams' closet, briefcase, and files.

"Something's amiss! All the papers are torn!" exclaimed Kyle.

Nats and I hastened to examine what he was referring to. "Look, several of these documents have been ripped," Kyle pointed out.

"Barely, it's just a small piece," I replied.

"But still, isn't it peculiar?" asked Kyle.

"Kyle, stop wasting our time like this! If you find something significant, let us know," instructed Officer Jones.

"Fine! Hmph," puffed Kyle, continuing his search through the files.

"I found it!" yelled Kyle ecstatically at the top of his lungs.

"It better be worth the time," replied Nats.

"It is! Quick, everyone come over!" urged Kyle.

"Except you, Wayne. George, come here! Take Wayne to the farthest room from here!" directed Officer Jones, who didn't seem to trust Wayne completely yet. George, one of the cops, promptly escorted Wayne to another room.

"Take a look! It's some kind of letter with burn marks on it. I suspect Mr. Williams had written a message, which the culprit burned and tore to shreds. We only have a small fragment of it," Kyle explained.

"Let me read it out!" said Nats, taking the fragment from him. "E did pie-pierce me. Hope this gets you closer to her accomplices. There's more, but it's torn," Nats read aloud.

"Wayne is innocent, then. It's a woman who attempted the

murder. That's very helpful, but I wish he had mentioned her name at the end as well," I commented.

"But why did you read it as 'E did pierce me'?" inquired Kyle. "I can't make out the letter before that," replied Nats.

"The word that's missing is 'she' because he mentions later-'her accomplices'," explained Officer Jones.

"He must have cleverly written a long letter revealing everything in case he died, and the woman must have burnt the evidence and torn it apart. Luckily, she couldn't hide this properly, which means that there are other fragments as well," explained Officer Jones.

"But she could've burnt the entire letter, but she didn't. Why?" I wondered.

"Well, even criminals make mistakes, as everything can't go perfectly in murder attempts. There's a possibility that she was running late and had to leave because someone was about to enter the Mayor's room," Officer Jones guessed.

"Probably, but why did he underline the word 'pierce'?" I asked after reading the message.

"I'm not too sure either. I'm guessing he wanted us to know that the lady carried a sharp object?" answered Nats doubtfully.

"Hmmm... but we already know that from seeing his wound. It isn't that; it's something he left for us to figure out," I responded.

"We should go and interrogate Jade McCallen since we now know that the culprit was a woman," suggested Officer Jones.

"I told you Jade could be the one, and afterward, we should

interview Sassy Granny also," suggested Nats.

"Who's 'Sassy Granny'?" asked Officer Jones.

"It's nothing, just an old lady who brought a strange-smelling medicine to the party, and Natasha suspected her to be the criminal," explained Kyle.

"Ah, I see, but we can't jump to conclusions like that," Officer Jones cautioned.

"I have a lot more evidence against her. First, she-" began Nats, but Officer Jones interrupted.

"We'll deal with this later. Let's go and apprehend Jade McCallen before she gets away. Now that we're sure the criminal is a woman, we should act swiftly. And none of you should breathe a word about the letter or the fact that the murderer is a woman. No one should know!" ordered Officer Jones sternly.

"Well, Officer, if you yell like that, there's no point in keeping it under wraps. Everyone is bound to find out," replied Nats.

"Shouldn't we search for more fragments around ?" asked Kyle.

"Kyle, we did look for it everywhere but couldn't find anything. If we don't act fast, she might escape," I explained.

"Ugh! Let's just go!" instructed Officer Jones, and we followed him out of Mr. Williams' house again!

CHAPTER 18
The Mayor's Past

"I wonder how Jade will react when she sees the cops," pondered Kyle.

"She'll pretend to be shocked but not worried," replied Nats.

"No need to speculate on that; we've arrived," declared Officer Jones.

"Does everyone remember the plan?" I reiterated, ensuring clarity.

"Yes," Nats replied, her annoyance evident.

As Officer Jones strode ahead, he rang the doorbell repeatedly.

"I'm coming!" yelled Jade from inside and flung the door open in annoyance.

"What's going on? Officer Jones, why are you here?" asked Jade with surprise.

"We're here for an interrogation. You see, your friends aka the other members of the Welfare Committee, were found with belongings of the Mystery Woman who wasn't present during the security check. So, we decided to interrogate even the Head of the Welfare Committee for any information against the ones found culpable," explained Officer Jones without revealing his true intentions.

"I do not have any evidence against them. They were found guilty? How is that possible?" asked a bewildered Jade or she pretended to be confused.

"The cops found the Mystery Lady's attire in their flats," I replied with disappointment.

"Shelly, dear! I had no idea! No wonder they weren't responding to my texts. But what brings you on an interrogation against your mom and her friends?" asked Jade cleverly, catching me off guard. I paused, not expecting to be confronted with this question. The plan seemed to be falling apart! Thinking quickly, I responded, "I know it seems odd, especially regarding my mom. But I asked Officer Jones to join the investigation team, and if I bail out now, it would breach his trust. I persuaded him that someone planted those items in Mom's, Trina's, and Courtney's apartments."

"Oh, I see. Well, come on in," said Jade, exhibiting a vague feeling of discomfort that I could discern. After settling into her living room, Officer Jones inquired, "Where were Courtney, Trina, and Grace at seven?"

"Courtney, Trina and I were dancing to the music when a waiter approached us and handed us masks. Grace had a terrible tummy ache, so she was in the washroom," replied Jade.

"How long was Grace in the bathroom?" asked the first cop.

"I don't know; I didn't keep track of the time," Jade replied.

"But I do know. I went to check on her. It took her about fifteen minutes, as she struggled to find an unoccupied one," I added.

"Fine, Grace is innocent. What about Trina and Courtney?" asked Officer Jones.

"They were with me all the time! They couldn't have done it," Jade insisted.

"You're right, they are not responsible. But what if they had someone else wear the outfit and planted the items in Grace's house to cast suspicion on you?" asked Officer Jones, subtly changing the course.

"What, no way! They aren't guilty! If you show me a picture of that lady's outfit, I can confirm if anyone has any of those items," assured Jade. The second cop presented his phone, and Jade's expression remained devoid of surprise.

"They don't even have clothes like that! In fact, they don't own anything that fashionable!" she replied.

"If that's the case, we'll take your word for it. We'll believe those three are innocent. But what about you? You were the only one without a single item from that lady's outfit," Officer Jones got straight to the point.

"I see, you came here on the pretext of suspecting them, but you are really here to interrogate me! Well played," Jade replied sharply.

"We're doing this because your own friend suspects you!" Nats blurted out.

"And who might that be? Trina, that immature jerk?" Jade snapped angrily.

"How did you know?" I inquired.

"Just because I disagreed with one of her suggestions about Green Avenue today, she's in a foul mood," Jade explained.

"What do you mean? She's your friend; she wouldn't hold a grudge for no reason," Kyle chimed in.

"She's notorious for holding grudges. Maybe I turned down one of her ideas before Kayla's party, or maybe even earlier? I can't recall, but she remembers them vividly," Jade revealed.

"You know what? I see why you're all doing this! It's because I'm friends with Juliette, and Juliette is close to Henry! Just because of that, you suspect me? You're no better than Mr. Gary, who falsely arrested the three of you!" Jade declared, glaring at Nats, Kyle, and me.

"It's not entirely because of that, Jade. Well, you're right, it is definitely because of that," I admitted.

"Shelly! You spoiled the-" Kyle started to say, but I cut in, "It's okay guys. Jade's clever enough to see through it. I apologize for the rough interrogation. I hope you'll allow us to continue for Mr. Williams' sake?"

"I don't want to, but I'll have to, for Henry and Grace, and to clear my name. But I must say, I'm disappointed in you, Shelly, for suspecting me in the first place," Jade replied. I remained silent in embarrassment but regained composure , knowing I had acted with good intentions.

"Is Juliette Clover really innocent?" asked Nats.

"She most definitely is, and I hope you believe me! She loved

Henry deeply, even knowing his heart belonged to Grace," replied Jade.

"What if Grace was pretending to love Henry to harm him?" asked the first cop who hadn't accompanied us to the precinct, which infuriated me.

"How dare you? Grace loved him genuinely!" I retorted.

"Don't worry, Shelly, I got this. Grace is so kind-hearted that she even urged Henry to either be honest with Juliette about their affair or break up with her for the sake of Juliette! Her love was genuine!" assured Jade. I mouthed a thank you to Jade, and she gave me a smirk, but I brushed it off.

"She should not have gotten involved in the first place!" replied the first cop who was persistent on assigning blame.

"She didn't intend for any of this to happen, but circumstances led them to fall in love. He had approached her," Jade explained.

"George, it's pointless to point fingers without evidence," replied Officer Jones to continue the planned interrogation.

"Understood, Sir! My apologies! I was just following previous plan, so I cooked something up," George apologized.

"You're quite skilled at manipulation, then! Had quite a scheme for my interrogation, huh?" Jade remarked, but no one responded.

"Let's move past this. Ask your next question," Jade said, visibly annoyed.

"How can you justify that you aren't the culprit? There are numerous leads against you. For instance, you want us to believe that your friends are innocent and someone planted the Mystery Woman's belongings in their homes, correct?" asked Officer Jones.

"That's correct," replied Jade.

"If that's the case, then there must be one person who had access to Trina, Grace, and Courtney's keys, and that person is none other than you!" declared Officer Jones. Jade's complexion paled, and she faltered for a moment.

"You have to trust me, Officer! Yes, I do have access to their keys, but it wasn't me! Right after the party at my place, I didn't leave my house. I stayed here the whole time! I didn't even know about the house checks!" she justified.

"You could've enlisted an accomplice to do the job. You were the only one who knew the exact spots to hide the mask and cloak in Trina and Grace's flats. You would know the places in their closets that they rarely check. What about that, huh?" asked Officer Jones.

"It wasn't me! And I don't know anything about their closets! I know who's behind this!" Jade insisted.

"Who is it?" asked Kyle.

"It's someone from Henry's past, someone dangerous," Jade speculated.

"Just tell us everything!" urged Nats.

"Fine, it's Henry's adversary, a formidable foe," Jade revealed.

"What's his name? Mr. Williams mentioned someone who attempted to steal Cool Inc.," I added.

"I can't disclose his name, and Officer Jones will agree with me on that," she replied firmly.

"I've heard murmurs about this dangerous individual, but I don't know his name," Officer Jones admitted.

"But why can't you?" I inquired.

"Because if his supporters catch wind of any negative talk about him, they can retaliate. They are a dangerous lot, and thanks to Mr. Williams, he was apprehended or something," Jade explained.

"Mr. Williams seemed uneasy discussing him. What exactly transpired with this individual?" I asked.

"He vanished from the Green Avenue abruptly after a case was filed against him. We're unsure of his fate, but I believe he was arrested. Only Henry knows the full story but remains tight-lipped about this sensitive issue," Jade elaborated.

"When Gary questioned the guests about Mr. Williams' adversary, none of them spoke up. They claimed he had no enemies," Officer Jones remarked.

"Well, that's because Henry instructed all of us not to talk about him ever again! The dangerous guy threatened Henry and his entire family once, and from that day on, Henry cautioned us against him for our own good," replied Jade.

"Why didn't anyone mention such a significant detail? I understand that the guy was a criminal, but by keeping silent about him, we won't be able to apprehend the real culprit," said Kyle.

"They were terrified! Not only did he threaten Henry, but he also made attempts on his life! That's why there's such a heavy guard presence outside his house. Initially, Henry even had CCTV cameras installed in his own room, but after the disappearance of the culprit in question, he assumed everything was secure and had them removed. Clearly, that wasn't the case," Jade explained with a tone of concern.

So, do we need to track down this individual or supporter of Mr. Williams' adversary who would have probably tried to kill the Mayor while the party was on? Kyle inquired.

"Yes, it's a big task, but we can rely on Jade's assistance for that," Officer Jones replied.

"Tell us more about him!" exclaimed Nats.

"He attempted to usurp control of Henry's company, despite Henry being the sole founder. This individual didn't contribute to Cool Inc.'s establishment whatsoever, yet deceitfully claimed he was a co-founder alongside Henry. While his name doesn't appear in any official records as a founder, he was adamant about gaining control. Under the guise of friendship, he fabricated a close bond with Henry and asserted they started the company together. However, Henry eventually ousted him. When Henry exposed his deception to the public, the adversary retaliated by threatening to kill Kayla and hurt Henry's family. However, before he could enact any harm, he vanished without a trace," Jade elaborated.

"How many years ago did he disappear?" I asked.

"About three years ago," she replied.

"Does this guy have any family members still residing in Green Avenue?" asked Officer Jones.

"No, I believe they relocated around the time of his disappearance. Some speculated he might be deceased, but Henry informed us he was arrested," replied Jade.

So, there's no one left here? Do you have any contact information for his relatives or family?" Nats asked.

"I never associated with him personally. In fact, I never even spoke to him. However, I recall he mentioned his mother being around. Despite being a bachelor and almost the same age as Henry, in his early thirties at the time, he audaciously deceived Henry. But as far as his mother is concerned, she never visited him here," Jade revealed.

"His mother didn't live here?" I clarified.

"No, she didn't. She never visited him," Jade added.

"So, no one can confirm her identity?" Nats questioned.

"None of us ever laid eyes on her. However, Henry casually mentioned his adversary spoke of his mother, whose name apparently is Adel. Given the animosity between Henry and his adversary after the attempted company takeover, it's plausible someone from his family could be behind the recent threats. With the Mystery Woman's appearance, I strongly suspect Adel may be the culprit," Jade concluded.

"Adel, hmmm... roughly how old would you say she was?" asked Nats.

"I couldn't say for sure, but given that he was in his early thirties, I'd estimate she was in her late fifties. So, by now, she'd likely be in her sixties," Jade answered.

"Do you know how to spell her name? Is it A-D-E-L?" I asked for clarification.

"I believe so, but I'm not certain about the exact spelling," Jade admitted.

"But I doubt this is the work of his enemy's mother. My intuition tells me it's someone with a grudge against the Welfare Committee. They deliberately placed the Mystery Woman's attire in the flats of Welfare Committee members, except for Jade's, to incriminate her. Do you have any suspects in mind?" Kyle asked cleverly.

"There's one woman who vehemently opposes our work, and that's Lydia," Jade revealed.

"I had a hunch! I knew that Sassy Granny was involved in some way!" yelled Nats.

"But how could she have gotten hold of their keys?" I asked.

"Perhaps she used the pin trick Kyle talked about," Nats suggested.

"Possible, but could she move fast enough to access their flats and return before the house checks? No one was aware of the plan, so how would she know Courtney had gone out or the contents of Trina and Mom's closets?" I questioned.

"In that case, it might not be Lydia. Are there any other individuals who dislike the committee?" Kyle inquired.

"There are several others, but listing them all would take quite some time," Jade replied.

"Perhaps we should focus on locating his mother then," I suggested.

"Oh boy, that will be such an easy task!" remarked Nats sarcastically.

"Do you have any additional information about him? Was he close enough to Mr. Williams to be familiar with the layout of his house?" I inquired further.

"He was very, very close to him. I guess he frequented Henry's residence many times. If it helps, I can provide a physical description," suggested Jade.

"While it may not be immediately useful, please go ahead," Nats encouraged.

"He's tall and slender, with straight black hair and a fair complexion. Back then, he was a fervent Yankees supporter, though I'm unsure if that's still the case. He used to attend all their games and had a passion for baseball in general," Jade described.

"Did you mention straight black hair?" Nats confirmed.

"Yes, that's correct," Jade affirmed.

"Then it's either his mother or his sister!" Nats concluded.

"It's his mom or his sister then!" cried Nats.

"What are you talking about?" asked Kyle.

"The Mystery Woman's identity. In the video, she had straight black hair, just like Mr. Williams' enemy!" clarified Nats.

"While I'm not certain about his sister, it's plausible it could be his mother," Jade added.

"But hold on, we shouldn't rush to conclusions and waste time. What if it was merely a wig?" I questioned.

"But what if it wasn't? Sometimes, a bit of imagination is necessary in such situations, Shelly," Nats countered.

"Okay, let's assume she's his mother, but we only know her name is Adel, and we're unsure of the spelling," I reminded them.

"Thank you, Jade, for providing such detailed information about the Mayor's adversary. None of our other interviews yielded anything nearly as informative. You are brave and, for now, consider you innocent," stated Officer Jones.

"No problem, even if you don't declare me innocent, because I have nothing to hide," replied Jade with a smile.

"Wait a moment, Jade!" I said just before we left. "Is Mr. Williams' enemy named Pierce?" I asked.

Jade's face turned pale as paper, and she stood there in stunned disbelief, gazing at me.

CHAPTER 19
Sassy Granny's turn

"Is she correct?" asked Nats. Jade didn't reply, but we figured that the individual in question was indeed Pierce. Unable to contain his curiosity, Officer Jones pressed on,"Jade, is his name Pierce? Hello, are you there?"

"Yes, it is him, but how did you know that? His name was removed from all the sites on the internet!" exclaimed Jade.

"Because Mr. Williams had written a note stating who the killer was, but that was torn into pieces. The only legible piece of information was one stating that he was pierced, and the word 'pierce' was underlined," I explained.

"Oh, I see, that's clever! No wonder he stressed on that word!" remarked Kyle.

"What's his full name?" asked Nats.

"I can't say. His family could do anything to me!" replied Jade.

"Tell us, or we'll hold you accountable for this!" threatened Officer Jones.

"You can't! You don't have proof!" replied Jade.

"It doesn't matter! You knowing his name and being paranoid shows that you are guilty in some way or the other," added Nats.

"I won't say anything!" cried Jade.

"Just tell us! Do you want your friends to be framed for no reason?" I urged.

"No, I don't want that but-" she started to say, when Kyle implored softly,"Jade, please! Just tell us quietly; it's not like there are cameras in your house."

"There might be, you never know!" replied Jade cautiously.

"Spill the beans!" ordered Officer Jones.

"It's...... Pierce Ackleman," she finally revealed.

"I'll try to find out something about him," I declared.

"It's futile. A few agents made sure there wasn't a shred of information about him," she replied.

"But still, there must be something. Whose agents were they?" I questioned.

"I'm not entirely sure. I believe they were government agents who recognized the threat Pierce posed after Henry's case," answered Jade.

"Thanks for the information, Jade. Officer Jones, I think we should proceed to the next interrogation," Nats reminded.

"Oh, yes! Thank you again, Jade. And if you recall anything else about him, please don't hesitate to let us know," Officer Jones stated.

"Before we leave, could you please provide us with directions to Lydia's place?" I asked.

"But doesn't Mr. Jones already know her address because he was a part of the house checks?" asked Jade.

"I wasn't; it was my team, and when they informed me about the things they found in Grace, Courtney, and Trina's houses, I stepped in," replied Officer Jones.

"Where is it?" Nats asked, her eyes filled with anticipation and curiosity.

"It's just opposite to mine. The one with the black door," she said, gesturing toward a flat with a hideously ugly entrance and décor, complete with black magic charms.

"We're heading there!" declared Nats.

"Okay, then! And please remember to let out my friends!" she said.

"Got it!" said Officer Jones, and we left. As we walked towards Lydia's flat, Kyle asked, "Shell, what are you doing?"

"I was just trying to look up Pierce," I answered.

"Do it later when you have time. Right now, we have to interrogate Lydia, whom Natasha suspects," instructed Officer Jones.

"But Officer, that isn't true! You'll see when we interrogate her. She's just quirky, not guilty," I explained.

"We can never be too sure, can we?" asked Officer Jones.

I locked my phone and went to knock on her door. I knocked once, but there was no response. The second time I knocked, I noticed someone peeping through the window, but no one opened the door. At last, I called for Lydia to come out.

"We know you're in there, Lydia! Come out, open the door!" I yelled out of frustration. A shadow approached the door and opened it rather slowly. It was Lydia, but she seemed annoyed.

"What the hell do you want?" she asked.

"Ma'am, I understand that you're a senior citizen, but that doesn't mean you have the authority to be rude to others! I'm the head of the NYPD, and I have personally come to interrogate you," stated Officer Jones.

"Why again? Wasn't that brat Gary's interrogation enough?" asked Lydia, totally ignoring what Officer Jones had just said about being rude.

"We have to do it again because Gary didn't do it properly," replied Kyle.

"Is it because of that mean brat that you think I'm guilty?" asked Sassy Granny, pointing to Nats.

"Sort of... but that doesn't matter now, Sassy Granny. Make a conscious effort not to look guilty. That's advice to you from my side, and besides, I have my reasons to feel that you're related to the crime. We aren't saying that you are guilty, but we just want to interrogate you once again," explained Nats.

"Why are you listening to this brat, Officer? I'm innocent, and that's the truth. I don't need to prove that to some motley crew," stated Sassy Granny and was about to close the door when Officer Jones stopped it with his hand, and it flew open. It was like a scene straight out of a movie where the hero showcases his strength.

"Enough is enough! We're coming in, and you have no choice but to answer our questions," said Officer Jones and urged us to enter as well. Nats went in excitedly, and Kyle and I reluctantly followed into Sassy Granny's flat. The decor of her flat matched the entrance's, which wasn't a shock to me knowing her. If I had to compare her flat to someone's, I would probably compare it to a witch's. Officer Jones and Nats sat on the only two chairs in her house, which forced Kyle and me to sit on her only messy couch along with her. Kyle gave me the 'why should we sit next to her' look, to which I reacted with the 'cut it out, we don't have a choice' look. Sassy Granny sat next to us with a grumpy expression on her face.

"We shall begin the interrogation now!" declared Officer Jones.

"Where were you at seven o' clock? We bumped into you at around ten minutes to seven while looking for Mrs. Peterson, but where did you go after that?" asked Nats like a true detective, stating all the facts. She even looked the part, wearing a detective cap for this interrogation.

"Ugh! I don't remember, okay! After telling you where Grace went, I went to the place where everyone had been gathered for the masquerade ball announcement," replied Sassy Granny.

"But after that, when we returned at around seven twenty, you weren't there, which was right after Mr. Williams' attempted murder. Where did you disappear for half an hour?" questioned Nats.

"After hearing the announcement, I went to the north zone to see what was brewing there," answered Sassy Granny calmly.

"Are you sure you went to the north zone? Because Trina and Courtney don't remember you being there?" asked Nats.

Sassy Granny's countenance betrayed a subtle expression of shock. "I was there. They probably didn't see me because I was at the back, trying not to bump into troublesome children," Sassy Granny retorted, roasting Nats.

"Argh! That's not the point! The point is that you weren't in the north zone at seven-fifteen, the time when the Mayor was stabbed. Where were you then?" Nats pressed again.

"How do you know whether I was there or not? Weren't you in the bathroom talking to Grace around that time?" questioned Sassy Granny.

"No, that was a little after seven. After that, we met Mrs. Peterson at around seven-twenty, and you weren't there then. We spotted you a little before eight. Where were you from seven-twenty to eight?" Nats inquired.

"I was among the people in the ball," she answered.

"Oh really? Because you weren't there when we danced the entire time, and the ball happened at the centre of the ground floor, not in the north, south, west, or east wings individually," Nats pointed out.

"I don't need to justify myself to a nasty brat. I was there, and you couldn't notice me as I don't have a large stature," she replied.

"Okay, fine! We'll believe that you were there the entire time, but why did you lie that Mrs. Peterson went towards the south when she was in the bathroom in the south wing?" asked Nats.

"Why is she the only one asking all the questions?" Sassy Granny questioned.

"That's because she has noticed a few things about you that we haven't," replied Officer Jones.

"Kyle and I never suspected you, but we're doing this out of formality," I stated, though Sassy Granny didn't seem too pleased.

"Will you please answer the question, Ma'am?" Nats sarcastically asked.

"Now you're being too respectable, calling me 'Sassy Granny' all this time! Anyways, I'll answer the question and get this interrogation over with. I lied for fun! I mean, why should you get things the easy way? You should do it yourself," she replied.

"Spooning information, huh? Seriously? They just asked where Grace went, and you think that's spoon-feeding? Gosh! You are weird!" Officer Jones remarked.

"Officer, can I talk to you for a moment?" Nats asked, and Officer Jones and she stepped out of Lydia's flat. "You guys get going too," urged Sassy Granny.

"Nope, we'll be here because I have one question for you," I replied.

"What is it?" asked Sassy Granny in a vinegar tone.

"Did you happen to see this lady in the south wing?" I asked, showing the pic of the Mystery Woman. Lydia saw it for a second, tried to jog her memory, and then she said, "Nope, never saw her! Such a weird outfit!" she remarked.

"She's all clear!" declared Kyle. When I turned back, I noticed Nats and Officer Jones smiling, and they were coming back. Knowing Nats, she didn't give up on this interrogation and must have planned to extract more info.

"Can we please have a glass of water?" asked Nats innocently.

"Just go to the kitchen and open the third drawer from the top and then---" said Sassy Granny when Officer Jones intervened, "I don't think it is right to enter someone's kitchen. It's better if you get it...I don't think you'd be comfortable if we just go in there."

"Fine, hmph!" said Sassy Granny and left the living room. Just as she left, Nats grinned and casually went into Sassy Granny's room. Officer Jones whispered, "Don't act suspicious. Natasha is onto something, and I'm going to distract Lydia for a while now. Be quiet, especially you, Kyle!" Kyle and I were clueless about what would happen next.

"Excuse me, Lydia, I've come to give you a hand. It was wrong of me to let you get water for all of us. I'll do it," insisted Officer Jones.

"Now you're coming to help me? You should've realized it back then! I won't leave because I don't trust you with my kitchen," replied Sassy Granny.

"It's just water! I'm not making coffee," said Officer Jones.

"But you can go now!" yelled Sassy Granny. Officer Jones left the kitchen and continued to distract Lydia. After two minutes, Nats returned with Lydia's phone!

"What did you do?" I asked her softly.

"Nothing, I got her phone," said Nats, stating the obvious.

"We know that, but why?" asked Kyle.

"To search for clues," replied Nats.

"Aren't you going too far?" I asked.

"No, I'm not! She is definitely the murderer, and I'm gonna prove it!" declared Nats.

"Let's see, if you don't, we aren't gonna tell you anything about what we found out," I threatened her.

"Did you find out anything? I don't think so," mocked Nats.

"She ain't wrong," stated Kyle.

"I know that Kyle, but we'll find something soon," I replied.

"You're optimistic now?" asked Nats.

"Yes, I just became! You can go on with your drama, but I'm sure it isn't worth it," I remarked. This was the first time in so many years that Nats and I broke into a fight.

"Leave it, Shell, don't fight over this," said Kyle.

"But she can ruin someone's life, Kyle," I explained.

"I won't! Trust me, I know what I'm doing," insisted Nats and left us. Sassy Granny came at last with the glasses of water. I stood up, took the glasses from her, and thanked her.

"Is my interrogation done?" asked Sassy Granny.

"Any questions?" Officer Jones asked Kyle and me.

"I do have one question," I added.

"This is the last one, right?" she asked.

"Yes, it is. I realized that you live right opposite Jade, so I wanted to ask whether you saw her put the belongings of the Mystery Woman in her friends' flats?" I asked.

"What belongings?" asked Sassy Granny ignorantly.

"That lady's outfit. She had worn a cloak, a gown, and a mask, and those were found in three different people's flats during the house checks. So I'm asking if you saw Jade going out of her house with those?" I questioned.

"I don't look out of the window like others do. I have other things to do, such as look after my cats," she explained.

"You have cats in there?" asked Kyle.

"Yeah, I do. They're sleeping inside, but you aren't allowed," she stated.

"Where is that nasty girl?" asked Sassy Granny, noticing that Nats wasn't there.

"She went out as she got a call," I replied, cooking up an excuse.

"A call, hmm... That reminds me, I didn't check my phone in a long time," said Sassy Granny and went into her room to look for it. "Looking for this?" asked Nats, showing Sassy Granny her phone.

"You witch! How dare you?" she yelled.

"How dare you utter 'how dare you' to me! Do you know what I'm implying here? If you do, you better come clean right now!" cried Nats.

"What's going on?" I asked calmly, maintaining my composure.

"Oh, it has nothing to do with you, Shelly. Thank me later," Nats replied ambiguously.

"Return my phone!" Sassy Granny screamed.

"I will give it back to you. I'm coming for you," Nats said stealthily, in a tone that made me feel uncomfortable.

"You better give it right now!" cried Sassy Granny. Nats quietly walked towards Lydia with the phone in her hand. She walked and stood close to her, pausing for a moment. Lydia grew impatient and came closer to Nats. Suddenly, Nats stretched her hand out and pinned Lydia against the wall. Sassy Granny was startled and yelled, "What's wrong with her? How can you be so mannerless?" Nats ignored her screams and exerted force to prevent Lydia from escaping. Lydia desperately tried to push Nats' hand away, but it was of no use.

"How are you so strong?" asked Kyle.

"Along with parkour, I'm proficient in karate too. Did you forget?" replied Nats. Lydia bit Nats' hand but she didn't seem to care about it.

"What's happening?" asked Officer Jones.

"Lydia, you always hated it when I called you 'Sassy Granny', right?" asked Nats, totally ignoring Officer Jones' question.

"I asked you a question, Natasha!" stated Officer Jones firmly. Nats didn't even look at him and said, "I asked you a question, Lydia! Reply to it or I'll be here all day, and you'll be tired, but I won't. I'll even adapt to your flat."

"Why won't I hate the name 'Sassy Granny'? It's disrespectful to your elders!" cried Sassy Granny.

"Very well, then! I won't call you 'Sassy Granny'. Instead, I have a new name for you. Wanna guess?" asked Nats in a seductive tone.

"Officer, help me out! Arrest this mad girl!" yelled Lydia.

"Enough, Natasha! Stop it!" cried Officer Jones.

"Since Officer Jones is being impatient here, I'll cut to the chase. I have a new name for you, and I hope you like it. From now on, I won't call you 'Sassy Granny' anymore, Lydia, or should I say, Adel Ackleman!" said Nats, pinning her with both hands instead of one.

CHAPTER 20
Nats' wild accusation

I was taken aback by Nats' statement, but I believed she might have been confused. Sassy Granny, on the other hand, remained calm and silent, reinforcing my suspicion that Nats had messed up. Was she implying that Lydia was Pierce Ackleman's mom?

"Haha! Aren't you a little too foolish?" asked Sassy Granny casually, as if nothing had happened.

Nats was shocked after her reaction. "But how did you think that she was Adel?" asked Kyle.

"How can you laugh, witch? Adel, reply! And Kyle, I don't believe it, I frigging know it!" cried Nats.

"I'm not Adel, stupid. Take her to the mental hospital, Officer," suggested Sassy Granny.

"Natasha, I don't know how you think that she's Adel, but seriously, girl, you really need to go there!" joked Officer Jones.

"When Shelly found out the identity of----" replied Nats when I reminded her, "You cannot tell his name! It's a secret!"

"Okay, but when she told his name, all of you believed her, but why not me? I'll tell you everything but I won't let her go, even if you beg me to!" declared Nats.

"Fine, tell us why you think she's Adel Ackleman," I said.

"'Cause I saw a notification on her phone!" yelled Nats.

"And?" I asked.

"That person called her 'Adel'!" declared Nats.

"Wait, she is right then!" declared Officer Jones.

"Oh, Adel was my old name. I changed it legally in my forties, but she doesn't know it," replied Sassy Granny.

"Doesn't that sound too farfetched? She's lying!" stated Nats.

"Why didn't you tell us about this before?" asked Officer Jones.

"Why should I? This was a long time ago, and you never asked me what my name was; you asked me what my name is," emphasized Adel, no, Lydia, no, I'll stick to Sassy Granny. Anyways, after that, I decided to put the name topic on hold, and I asked, "Who messaged you?"

"I don't know 'cause that brat had my phone; let me go!" she replied.

"I won't! I'll show you her message, and you should tell her name at once!" threatened Nats and held the phone at a distance from Lydia.

"Oh, that's Tara," replied Sassy Granny casually.

"I know her name is Tara 'cause you literally named it like that!

I'm asking you to tell us how she is related to you," explained Nats.

"She's just my old buddy, my best friend, to be precise," she replied.

"If she's your best friend, then how the hell did she not know your new name?" asked Officer Jones flaring up suddenly.

"We lost touch and got our contacts back. I don't need to justify anything to you, even if you are the head of NYPD! I don't need to justify myself to God as well 'cause God doesn't exist! I'm not even answerable to myself! And I order you to get out of my house!" screamed Sassy Granny.

"Woah! Chill, Lydia! No one is accusing you, and the way you're acting right now, I believe Nats wasn't entirely wrong after all," remarked Kyle.

"I think Lydia here is trying to say that she isn't even that close to her best friend and now they're slowly catching up," I guessed.

"Not entirely true! I am close to her but because of a feud, she stopped talking to me. We were so close and are now so close that I would gladly consider her my sister!" replied Sassy Granny.

"Where does Tara live?" I asked.

"Lives in Jersey, and are you going to do a background check on her? Do not include her in this *** mess!" swore Sassy Granny angrily.

"Woah, woah, woah! We won't cross the limit like that. I just have one question for you, and that is...What's your last name, and can we see your birth certificate?" asked Kyle.

"I'm Lydia Miller, and I don't have my birth certificate with me, and I hope that you believe me," she replied in a subdued and vulnerable tone, which was unlike her.

"She's clear then!" declared Kyle.

"But do you remember seeing the Mystery Lady?" I asked.

"No, I never saw someone which such horrendous taste, not that the current generation has good taste or anything!" scoffed Sassy Granny.

"She is innocent, I guess. I'm so sorry, Officer Jones, Shelly, Kyle, and Sassy-Adel no, Lydia!" apologized Nats.

"I won't forgive you!" stated Sassy Granny and left instantly after Nats let her go.

"Seriously, Natasha? Why did you create such a ruckus just because her old name was Adel," said Officer Jones.

"That's it! I got it! We have to go back!" cried Nats.

"What happened? Tell us before you do anything drastic," insisted Officer Jones.

Nats whispered, "I just realized that Tara called Sassy Granny 'Aidyl' which was spelled as 'A-I-D-Y-L'! And doesn't that spelling ring a bell? It's LYDIA spelled backwards, dumb******"

"What are you saying?" I asked.

"Argh! It's tough to explain it! Just think about it this way, what if her name was Aidyl, and she's using an alias now?" explained

Nats.

We all stared at her as if she were speaking gibberish.

"Explain it to us," said Officer Jones.

"I'm implying that she said that her name was Aidyl and now it's Lydia, but what if her name was and has been Aidyl all this time, and she lied to us?" asked Nats.

"We can't suspect every single detail of her past, can we? If we do that, we'll go crazy and won't be able to find the criminal," replied Kyle.

"He's right, leave Lydia out of it," instructed Officer Jones.

"But, okay fine! She's innocent, happy?" grumbled Nats.

"Let's just go!" insisted Kyle and left instantly.

"Wait a sec, I don't have my phone with me! I think I left it at Sassy Granny's," stated Nats.

"Get it then and don't create a commotion," replied Officer Jones.

"Okay, Officer! Shelly, can you come along with me? I don't wanna go alone after what's happened," said Nats.

"Sure, I would love to!" I replied sarcastically.

Nats held my hand and walked quickly towards Lydia's flat and knocked on her door. Sassy Granny opened the door instantly and gave Nats the death stare.

"Why are you here?" she asked.

"I forgot my phone," replied Nats sheepishly, as she genuinely didn't want to cause inconvenience for Sassy Granny.

"Fine, come in!" she said and Nats went in. She looked for her phone on the couch and then walked towards the kitchen. Sassy Granny followed her wherever she went to make sure Nats wouldn't dig dirt from her belongings.

"It's not here! Oh my gosh! How will I live!?" exclaimed Nats.

"I can give you a ring if you'd like," I offered, and proceeded to dial her number. Surprisingly, her phone remained silent. "Why isn't my phone ringing?" panicked Nats. I stayed silent, observing Sassy Granny's frustration. "Found it!" Nats final exclaimed, and showed her phone. "Where was it?" asked Sassy Granny. "In my pocket, on silent mode! So stupid of me!" Nats admitted.

"I apologize for wrongly assuming you were part of the Ackleman family. You obviously can't be related to Pierce Ackleman; that guy is a jerk!" stated Nats. "He threated Mr. Williams' family and Kayla over a company that wasn't even his! Can you believe this guy? I'm sorry for thinking you were his mom! Pierce deserved to be arrested!" Nats passionately added. Sassy Granny's response was unexpected: "How dare you talk about Pierce like that!" I was stunned, but Nats just smiled.

"So, you are Pierce's mom after all!" I declared. "Just made it in time," smirked Nats, and I turned back to see Officer Jones and Kyle. "You knew about this?" I asked. "Yes, Natasha told me everything, but I didn't believe her. After much insistence, I decided to give her a chance to catch Lydia red-handed. I'm going to cuff her!" replied Officer Jones. "You aren't going anywhere!" said Nats, pinning Lydia against the wall. Surprisingly, Lydia didn't make an attempt to escape.

"You caught me, brat, and I give you credit for that! I never expected you to be a smart cookie," coolly replied Sassy Granny. "And Pierce didn't do anything wrong! I will not tolerate anything against him, even if it were to thwart my plans just like it did right now! You'll pay for it later, Natasha!" yelled Sassy Granny.

"Be careful, Nats! This old lady is crazy after all!" cautioned Kyle.

"Oh, you won't be able to tolerate what I'm gonna say about your beloved son! He is a **** jerk who could've killed Kayla years ago! Now, he faced the brunt of his vengeance through you, but it could've been Kayla! I don't like Kayla myself, but threatening a child is way out of the rules!" stated Nats.

"Like you follow the rules yourself, brat! And for your information, it was Henry who snatched Pierce's company! Pierce started Fashion N More! Henry changed its name to Cool Inc., and suddenly, he's been made the CEO of the company that Pierce had started! He stole it all! He left us broke! He ruined our lives!" screamed Sassy Granny.

"Officer Jones, we'll have to close the windows, or else everybody will get to know about the investigation, and I'm sure she has many accomplices," said Kyle. Officer Jones closed the windows and doors.

"We believe you," I reassured Sassy Granny.

"What! Mr. Williams is innocent! Shelly, what are you doing?" questioned Nats.

"I'm sorry, Nats but I can't let you take this investigation further. We're extremely grateful to you for catching the murderer, but a calm person can handle tough situations better," I explained.

"So, you want me to leave?" asked Nats angrily.

"No, I want you to stay, but just don't interrogate her," I requested.

Nats didn't say a word and stepped back. Officer Jones and Kyle praised her efforts, bringing a chair for her.

"Rest, Natasha! You did a splendid job!" said Kyle.

"But who'll pin her against the wall then?" asked Nats.

"That's my job!" replied Officer Jones with a wink.

"Got it! But shouldn't we take her to the precinct?" asked Nats, taking a seat.

"No, we must extract info first! And we don't have conclusive evidence against her," replied Officer Jones.

"Tell us everything about Henry," I instructed.

"Why didn't you try to escape, Lydia? Don't all crooks try to escape when they're caught?" asked Kyle.

"Kyle, whose side are you on?" asked Nats infuriatedly.

"I won't escape! I'm not like the conventional criminals, don't associate me with them! In fact, I'm going to reveal everything about Henry to you, and then, you won't even want to arrest me!"

"She can't escape as she's cuffed; so there's no use trying!" replied Nats.

Sassy Granny retorted savagely, "He asked why I didn't escape, not why I'm not trying! Right when I blurted out that Pierce was innocent, I could have escaped, but I chose not to!"

"Ugh! You!" Nats exclaimed in frustration.

"Henry, that jerk!" swore Sassy Granny.

"Are you done swearing?" I asked.

"No, there's gonna be a whole lot more, but you've got to bear with it, brats! Henry was never the founder of Fashion N More! This was Pierce's brainchild, and he became a millionaire within a year! After about five years, Henry approaches Pierce for a casual get-together. My son agreed, and Henry just blabbers about his crappy life to him instead of talking about the good old childhood memories!" explained Sassy Granny.

"Childhood memories?" I asked.

"Yes, they were best friends in high school and in college. After that, they went their separate paths. Anyways, he randomly narrates his awful life after college and puts forward a pitiful story. He knew very well that Pierce was a kind man and knew how to exploit him! Hearing about how Henry struggled financially, Pierce agreed to employ him in his company. Within six months, Henry approached him for a promotion and innocently, Pierce made him the CTO!" narrated Sassy Granny.

"What! Really?" I asked.

"After that, everything went downhill. Henry attained a substantial position in the company and took over it in no time. He got the support of Pierce's people and influenced them to go against him. Within two years, Pierce was fired and Henry became the CEO of Cool Inc. The company neither had Pierce nor the name Fashion N More that Pierce had chosen for it! Life had turned upside down and Pierce came to visit me more often. He was planning to move in with me but I urged him to not give up and fight for what was rightfully his! I wish I hadn't," said Sassy Granny and seemed to have almost broken down.

"What happened after that?" I asked, eager to continue without wasting any time.

"Pierce confronted Henry in front of his ex-colleagues and the board members! Things escalated quickly, and Henry found himself facing Pierce in court. They had a month to prepare and hire lawyers. Pierce, being Pierce, was already ready with everything beforehand. He had a solid plan and faced Henry a month later. On the first day of the trial, Pierce completely humiliated Henry! He even called to inform me about how well his case went. But the next day, Henry showed up at court, confident and seemingly well-prepared after the previous day's debacle. However, Pierce never arrived," explained Sassy Granny.

"He didn't? Were you there with him during the trial?" I asked.

"No, I wasn't, but I had planned to be. I received a call early in the morning from an unknown number. I rejected the call four times and answered on the fifth attempt, only to receive the shock of my life. Pierce had been found dead in his apartment," Sassy Granny recounted, her eyes welling up with tears.

"Wha-What! Pierce isn't alive? Jade told us he was in prison!" Kyle exclaimed.

"Even prison would have been better! My son was murdered by none other than Henry Williams!" yelled Sassy Granny.

"Are you certain it was him?" I asked calmly.

"Yes, it was! He smiled the entire time! When the doctors examined Pierce, they discovered he had been poisoned! That's when I recalled that a few of Pierce's ex-colleagues had invited him to dinner to discuss his courtroom victory over Henry. It was during that dinner that they poisoned my son!" Sassy Granny wailed.

"But you lack evidence, correct?" I pressed.

"Do you really believe Aidyl!? Mr. Williams is the kindest soul we've ever met! How can you continue to interrogate her about him?" asked Nats.

"I'm not lying, Natasha! It's the dreadful reality! I have never broken down in front of anyone, not even my own husband! Henry **** killed him!" swore Sassy Granny.

"I don't believe you either, Aidyl! I'm with Nats on this one! Shelly, you can't possibly believe that Mr. Williams killed Pierce, can you?" asked Kyle.

"You're making this difficult for me. I'm just conducting an investigation, and it's my duty as the investigator to remain neutral," I whispered to Nats and Kyle.

"Fine!" Kyle and Nats replied in unison. However, for some peculiar reason, I found myself believing Sassy Granny.

"Let's move on, shall we? What's your response, Aidyl?" I asked.

"You're right; I didn't have any evidence. But after the case closed, I found a letter in Pierce's apartment," Sassy Granny disclosed.

"What did it say? Why did you pause?" asked Nats impatiently.

"The letter read, 'Yes, he was killed!'" Sassy Granny revealed.

"That's horrible! Did you return to court afterward?" Kyle asked.

"I did, but they refused to listen to me! I felt that Henry had bribed the judge as well, and they weren't willing to entertain my claims!" Sassy Granny explained.

"What did you do next?" I prodded.

"What could I do should be your question. Well, I was helpless, as no one believed me! My life turned upside down, and I was completely shattered! I left New York immediately and vowed never to return unless I had taught Henry a lesson!" Sassy Granny cried.

"When did you start living in Green Avenue?" I asked.

"Just four months ago, right after Henry became the Mayor," she replied.

"Why exactly did he want to become the Mayor?" asked Officer Jones.

"He couldn't handle the stress after Pierce's death, which occurred approximately a year ago," she answered.

"But why did he choose to become the Mayor?" Officer Jones pressed further.

"He wanted to create a positive image of himself so that everyone would forget about the court case. He resigned from Cool Inc., claiming that Pierce had caused him a great deal of stress, and he decided to take a temporary break from the company," Sassy

Granny elaborated.

"I recall Mr. Williams mentioning that you were very upset with him as the Mayor. How did you risk opposing him? Couldn't he have recognized you as Pierce's mother?" Nats inquired.

"That's an excellent question, Natasha! I didn't look like this earlier. I looked like this," Sassy Granny said, pulling out a photo from her purse.

"That was quick!" remarked Kyle.

Nats' reaction to Aidyl's pic was astonishing. "What's up, Nats? You look like you've seen a ghost," I said.

"Take a look at this!" Nats exclaimed, showing us Aidyl's photo. Aidyl had undergone a remarkable transformation over the course of a year! Despite being over sixty, she appeared youthful, with blonde hair styled in beautiful curls that cascaded just below her shoulders. I know I shouldn't be saying this, but she looked stunning! And she was smiling—something I had difficulty imagining Sassy Granny doing. It was clear that she had changed due to unfortunate circumstances.

"You look so different! Sassy Granny, you were beautiful! Your disguise worked!" Nats complimented.

"I merely cut my hair and dyed it brown. That was my only disguise," Aidyl explained.

Nats didn't seem to comprehend that Aidyl had aged a lot after Pierce's murder. I believed Sassy Granny now. Mr. Williams was the bad guy and she was just an innocent victim of his crime.

"You aged because of what happened to Pierce?" asked Kyle,

somewhat believing her story.

"Yes! That's what I've been trying to convey all along! Pierce was murdered by Henry, who is now in a coma and will likely die soon!" Sassy Granny said, smiling.

"Do you believe me?" asked Sassy Granny in a drunkard's tone.

"Are you drunk Sassy Granny?" asked Nats.

"Maybe I am! Who cares?" Sassy Granny retorted, bursting into uncontrollable laughter like a madwoman.

"She's definitely intoxicated," Officer Jones confirmed.

"What should we do?" I asked.

Well, Aidyl Ackleman, do you admit to stabbing Henry Williams?" Officer Jones asked.

Sassy Granny stopped laughing and stared at Officer Jones for a moment before responding, "Hell yeah, I do!"

"Well, then, you're coming with me to prison," Officer Jones declared, leading her away.

"Officer, if you don't mind, may I return to Mr. Williams' residence? One of the waitstaff is an accomplice," I suggested.

"If one of them is an accomplice, why didn't you bring that person to me?" Officer Jones questioned.

"I didn't want to jump to conclusions as we did with Wayne," I explained.

"Aidyl, tell us the name of the waiter who was your accomplice" commanded Officer Jones.

"I don't remember the name! Hahaha, I'm under arrest now! Justice has been served for Pierce Ackleman!" Sassy Granny exclaimed, before disappearing into custody.

CHAPTER 21
Which waiter is it?

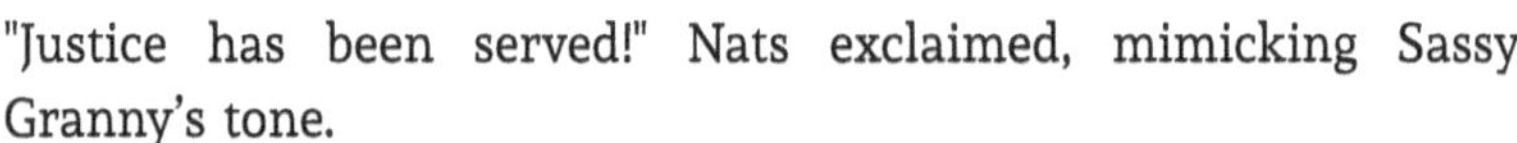

"Justice has been served!" Nats exclaimed, mimicking Sassy Granny's tone.

"Do you finally believe her?" Kyle inquired.

"Yeah, I do," Nats admitted softly.

"No need to feel ashamed about it," I reassured her.

"Truth be told, even I find myself believing her now," Kyle confessed.

"Ha! So, we're all on board with Granny's truth, then!" Nats declared triumphantly.

"I never explicitly said I believed her," I interjected.

"But you seemed inclined to believe her initially!" Nats countered.

"I was just trying to remain neutral. Anyway, let's focus and move on," I urged, shifting the conversation.

"Who is it, by the way?" Kyle inquired.

"That's classified. I want it to be suspenseful for you too. Let detective Shelly do her job!" I asserted.

"Fair enough," grumbled Nats and Kyle simultaneously.

After arranging an Uber, we hurriedly climbed into the cab and made our way to Mr. Williams' house, arriving in just ten minutes.

"Guys, wait! I have a few instructions," I announced.

"We should hurry before the suspect flees!" Kyle suggested urgently.

"Agreed, but let's act casual as we go upstairs, understood?" I confirmed.

"Got it," Nats replied, deliberately taking slow steps.

As we reached the top, Wayne approached me with a smile. "Everything's set, Ma'am, and now, I owe you one!"

"Well done, Wayne! Much appreciated," I replied, acknowledging his help before proceeding to the final room.

"Psst, Wayne!" whispered Nats.

"Yeah?" replied Wayne.

"Who's the suspect?" she asked in a hushed tone.

"I can't reveal that. Shelly instructed me not to, just in case she's mistaken. It could complicate things," Wayne replied discreetly.

"I can hear you, Nats!" I interjected.

"Ugh! Fine, you win," she grumbled.

"Let's see how it unfolds, Nats," Kyle chimed in.

We entered the room to find our suspect already seated.

"Oh, hi Rosa! What brings you here?" Nats asked innocently.

"I'm not sure, Wayne just told me to come," Rosa replied.

"Interesting," whispered Kyle.

"I wanted to discuss something with you, Rosa," I began.

"What is it?" she asked.

"I was just wondering— are you color-blind?" I inquired.

"Color-blind? No, why do you ask?" Rosa replied.

"Well, it's just that I noticed a couple of instances where you seemed to have trouble with colors," I explained.

"Oh, that's just a misunderstanding. I brought you the wrong bag because I was distracted, and that color game was confusing," Rosa defended herself.

"I understand, but why did you keep saying 'blue' instead of 'purple' during the game, even after being corrected?" I pressed.

"I guess I got mixed up. I read the word 'blue' instead of the color in which it was written!" explained Rosa.

"Let's try again then," I suggested, pulling out my phone. "I'll say the word, and you tell me the color."

"Alright, I got it," Rosa agreed.

"Blue," I said.

"Purple!" Rosa exclaimed.

"That's incorrect," I replied.

"But Shell—" Kyle began, before Rosa cut him off. "Okay, fine! I am color-blind. I didn't want it to affect my job," Rosa confessed.

"But how would that hinder your job as a waiter?" I asked.

"In a previous job, I had a mishap because of my color-blindness. I served the wrong person and got fired," Rosa explained.

"But in this case, you identified the color correctly," Kyle blurted.

"What?" Rosa looked surprised.

"Shelly tricked you into admitting your color-blindness," Nats chimed in.

"Wait, why would that matter for the crime?" Kyle asked.

"And why would a boss instruct waiters based on the color of their clothes instead of using table numbers?" I added.

"My old boss was just crazy, alright? He fired me over a silly mistake. He had a bad temper," Rosa defended herself.

"Yeah, there are some unreasonable bosses out there," I agreed. "But Rosa, how did you know the color of the Mystery Woman's dress if you're color-blind?"

Rosa hesitated, unable to respond.

"Maybe she just saw the Mystery Woman walk past and noticed the color," Kyle proposed.

"No, dummy! What Shelly means is, how could Rosa know the Mystery Woman wore purple if she can't even see colors properly?" Nats clarified bluntly.

"Whoa, Rosa, how did you know that?" asked Kyle.

"It's simple, I heard it from one of the other waiters," she replied.

"Who was it? Let's call them right away," said Nats.

"I honestly can't remember... maybe Aaron or Tom, I'm not sure," Rosa replied innocently.

"Come on, you must know! You remembered the color of the Mystery Woman's dress because you were involved in the crime, duh!" I pointed out.

"I'm telling you, I had nothing to do with it! You can't just accuse me like that," Rosa protested.

"Too late to play innocent now, buttercup. Lydia confessed to the crime," Nats stated firmly.

"Aidyl did? Gosh, I never would've guessed she was involved," Rosa exclaimed.

"Wait, who's Aidyl? We were talking about Lydia," I interjected.

"I said Lydia, not Aidyl," Rosa insisted.

"No, you definitely said Aidyl," Wayne corrected.

"Wayne, do it!" I instructed, and he promptly locked the door and dialed 911.

"You can't arrest me! You have no proof!" yelled Rosa, swearing at us in Spanish. I understood every word, as I'm fluent in Spanish.

"At least they didn't catch the real killer!" Rosa cried out.

"What? Did you say that intentionally, hoping someone who understands Spanish would think we arrested the wrong person?" I asked.

"You understand Spanish at that speed?" asked Rosa, astonished.

"Yeah, I'm fluent, even with native speakers," I replied.

"Was it true?" I pressed, but before she could answer, the police arrived and took Rosa away.

"What did she say?" asked Nats.

"She said we arrested the wrong person," I said solemnly.

"What? Isn't Aidyl the murderer?" asked Kyle.

"Not necessarily. She must have been an accomplice, which means the real killer is still out there," Nats concluded, her voice tinged with a sense of foreboding, like something out of a thriller movie.

CHAPTER 22
Someone's still out there

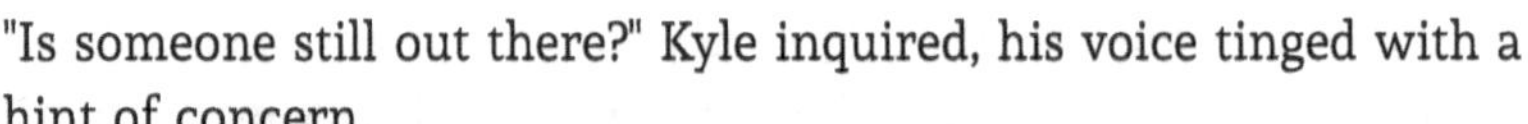

"Is someone still out there?" Kyle inquired, his voice tinged with a hint of concern.

"Yes," Nats and I replied simultaneously.

"Should we inform Officer Jones about it?" Kyle suggested.

"No, he's busy attending to Sassy Granny's situation," Nats replied.

"We aren't sure whether it was Aidyl or not because I might not have heard her correctly," I added.

"I'm pretty sure you did, 'cause Rosa was shocked that you understood her fast Spanish," Kyle interjected.

"I just hope it was Aidyl, 'cause it's a lot of work, honestly," I grumbled.

"Shelly, are you complaining? Wow, that's a first!" Nats remarked playfully..

"You're not helping, Nats!" I grumbled once again.

"Shelly, take a back seat for a while. Nats and I will handle it for now. You've slogged it out these last two days, and we need our sharpest brain at its best, don't we, Nats?" Kyle suggested.

"Yes, we do! Who cares if the murderer gets away with her crime? Our bestie's peace of mind matters more! Go home, and we'll discuss our leads with you tomorrow, okay?" Nats added.

"What? That doesn't even make sense!" I protested.

"You get the idea! Go, go!" urged Kyle.

"Are you sure you both will be able to handle this?" I asked.

"Yes, absolutely we will!" Nats assured with confidence.

"I'll be going then. When will both of you get home?" I inquired, eager to know their plans.

"In two to three, I guess. It's already five thirty!" Nats exclaimed.

"We did so many interrogations today!" Kyle added, reflecting on the day's events.

"No wonder time flew by so fast!" I remarked, realizing the intensity of our efforts.

"Before I go, what about Juliette?" I asked.

"What about her?" Kyle queried, prompting me to elaborate further.

"I mean when will she be back?" I clarified, seeking clarity on Juliette's whereabouts.

"She told me that she would come by seven," Nats replied.

"Oh, hasn't she been outside for too long?" I expressed concern.

"You're right!" agreed Kyle.

"Do you think she was the murderer?" Nats speculated.

"Quite possible, but let's wait and see. If she isn't back, call me!" I instructed.

"Sure!" they replied.

I left the room and descended the stairs, feeling a sense of relief wash over me. Finally, I could rest!

Upon reaching home, I dialed Officer Jones to inquire about Sassy Granny's situation. "What's up?" he greeted.

"Nothing much, Officer. I just wanted to check on how things are going there," I replied.

"Not much to report. She didn't protest and went in happily," he informed me.

"Officer, I hope you haven't disclosed Aidyl's arrest to the media. Please refrain from informing Mr. Williams' family or anyone else, as we've learned she isn't the killer but an accomplice," I urged.

"What?! Are you sure?" Officer Jones exclaimed, his disbelief evident.

"According to Rosa, yes," I confirmed.

"Good heavens!" he exclaimed. "Don't worry, Officer. Nats and Kyle are handling it. I'm heading home as I'm quite exhausted. I hope that's alright," I said.

"Absolutely! You're our best detective, even better than the one we had before! And I'll keep an eye on those two. I'm heading to Mr. Williams' house now," Officer Jones assured me.

"That means a lot, Officer! Thank you!" I expressed my gratitude.

"Alright then, I have to go now. Bye!" Officer Jones concluded, and the call ended.

After a twenty-minute walk, I arrived home feeling utterly drained. Mom greeted me at the door, and I was relieved to hear that she had been released.

"Shelly, they believed us!" Mom exclaimed happily.

"Yes, Mom! We convinced them, and we also apprehended two accomplices!" I announced proudly.

"Who are they?" Mom inquired softly.

"You won't tell anyone, right?" I asked for reassurance.

"Of course, I won't," Mom promised.

"Alright then. The first one is Lydia, and the other..." I began, but Mom interrupted with an astonished, "Holy cow!"

"Yeah, Nats suspected her from the start, but none of us believed her," I explained.

"And who's the other one?" Mom queried, her curiosity growing.

"Rosa, she's one of the waiters. You wouldn't know her," I replied.

Mom seemed visibly worried for some reason. "What's wrong, Mom? You seem troubled," I observed, sensing her unease.

"I'm concerned they might retaliate against you! People like them often seek revenge against those who impede their plans, or they might inform their accomplices about you, Natasha, and Kyle," Mom explained her apprehension.

"Relax, Mom. They're behind bars now, and the other accomplices will be terrified. But even if they try anything, I'll handle it," I assured her, hoping to alleviate her worries.

"Why don't you take a rest for a while, honey," Mom suggested, handing me some evening snacks to munch on.

Mom asked worriedly, "Where are Natasha and Kyle?" She had completely forgotten about them. "Oh, they're still at Mr. Williams' place. They suggested I take a break since I was exhausted after learning that Aidyl isn't the murderer," I replied. Mom was taken aback. "Then who is the murderer, and who's Aidyl?" she asked. "To make a long story short, Lydia's real name is Aidyl Ackleman. She was undercover as Lydia, the grumpy old lady whom everyone hates in the neighborhood," I explained.

Mom was even more shocked upon learning Lydia's full name. "I know you must be shocked that she is an Ackleman, but why didn't you tell me about Pierce Ackleman, Mom?" I asked.

"Darling, as precautions, we were forbidden to talk about the Ackleman family because, you might not know this, but Pierce threatened to kill Kayla," replied Mom.

"I do know about it, Mom, but you could have told me privately," I said.

"I was scared, okay! I was worried that his family might do something to the investigation crew. I know he's still in prison, but his family could have done something to you," added Mom.

"Mom, he's dead," I replied.

"What! I didn't know that!" said a startled Mom.

"Yeah, that's the only good thing. Do you think the murderer might be someone related to Pierce Ackleman?" I asked, for her instincts have an accuracy rate of ninety-nine-point nine nine percent.

"Hmmm…let's see. I'm guessing Lydia is related to him, 'cause her surname is Ackleman as well. What about that waitress Rosa?" asked Mom.

"All I know is that she's a Latina and I don't think she's related to Pierce. I forgot to tell you that Aidyl, aka Lydia, is none other than Pierce's mom," I disclosed.

"What!? That means that she must have killed Henry," replied Mom.

"We got to know that Lydia was just an accomplice and not the killer, which means that the crime hasn't been solved yet," I explained.

"This killer seems like a very dangerous person!" said Mom worriedly.

"Don't worry, Mom," I reassured.

"Please be careful, Shelly! You don't know what the Acklemans are capable of!" Mom informed.

"I'll be careful," I promised.

"Thank you! I'll take a nap as I'm feeling the blues," Mom said.

"You're going through a lot, Mom. Your lover is in a coma, and then you became a suspect for the police. Things have been wild," I said.

"Henry didn't have an affair with me," denied Mom shyly.

"Mom, it isn't bad, as he wasn't married to Juliette," I added gently, seeking to ease her guilt.

"Yes, you're right, I loved him! He was going to finish things with Juliette after Kayla's birthday but before that," replied Mom, her voice breaking as tears flowed freely.

"He didn't deserve it! The only reason he was engaged to Juliette was because Kayla admired Juliette and was extremely fond of her and saw her as a role model. Juliette took advantage of this and proposed to him, and he couldn't help but say yes for the sake of Kayla. I was mad at him and broke up with him. He promised me that he would end it in a week and before that, he was ...!" cried Mom, her emotions pouring out uncontrollably.

"I'm so sorry, Mom!" I replied.

Mom wailed, and I tried my best to comfort her. I had initially planned to offer words of consolation, to reassure her that Henry was the one at fault and that justice had been served. But as I witnessed the rawness of her pain, I found myself unable to utter those words. The extent of her love and the magnitude of her loss were too deep to find comfort in such simple reassurances. After what felt like an eternity, Mom stopped crying, and I enveloped her in a tender embrace, hoping to ease the ache in her heart. Soon after, I guided her to bed, much like she had done for me countless times when I was a child. Tucking her in, I watched over her as she drifted into an uneasy sleep.

An hour had passed, and Nats and Kyle still weren't home. I decided to call them for updates, my worry mounting with each passing minute. Nats picked up the phone, but I couldn't hear anything for a minute. "Hello? Hello?" I called.

"Shelly, we were just about to call you," replied Nats from the other end.

"Any updates?" I asked anxiously.

"Only two. Firstly, Ms. Clover has still not returned, and she's acting suspicious. Secondly, we got to know that the doctors are still trying to revive Mr. Williams. They sensed his heartbeat weakening second by second and are trying their best."

"But I think he'll be arrested for what he did," I replied.

"Oh yeah, I forgot about that," remarked Kyle.

"What's that noise, Shell?" asked Nats, her voice filled with curiosity.

"Oh, I'm outside. I'm taking a stroll, as Mom is exhausted and is sleeping, and I didn't want to disturb her with this call," I replied.

"Also, Officer Jones told us that the other cops informed him about the Pierce case, and they believe that it shouldn't be disclosed that Mr. Williams was almost murdered by an Ackleman or someone related to them," informed Kyle.

"Great! Kayla will go crazy otherwise," I replied, .

"Yup, so when are you coming?" asked Nats, redirecting the conversation.

"Do you want me to? Did you get any leads? Should I come?" I asked.

"Juliette hasn't returned, and Kyle and I suspect Juliette and Jade for many reasons," replied Nats.

"Why Jade?" I asked, my curiosity piqued by this new development.

"We know that the murderer is a woman, and the only ones who know the infrastructure of Mr. Williams' house and his schedule are Juliette and her good friend, Jade!" explained Nats, with sound reasoning.

"You are correct!" I agreed, my mind racing with the implications of their suspicions.

"Speaking of Juliette, she just arrived, so you don't need to come," informed Kyle.

"We'll head out now since she's back. Bye!" said Nats.

"Bye, and come soon!" I replied and ended the call.

After ten minutes, the doorbell rang, and I cursed them for not remembering that Mom was sleeping. I quickly opened it and glared at them.

"What?" asked Nats.

"Mom is sleeping, idiot," I reminded them.

"Sorry, anyways, did you rest?" asked Nats.

"Kinda. Anyways, did you guys find anything?" I asked, eager for any updates on our investigation.

"Not much, to be honest, but both of us suspect Juliette. When she came home, she wasn't that upset or gloomy. Jade could've easily placed the belongings in Courtney, Trina, and your Mom's closet and snitched on Sassy Granny to escape," explained Kyle.

"That totally makes sense, for some reason! But what is Jade's reason to kill Mr. Williams?" I questioned.

"Maybe she's just supporting Juliette to steal his money or something like that," suggested Nats.

"But why would Juliette be after money? Doesn't she have a lot already?" I asked, puzzled.

"Greed can never be satisfied," replied Kyle.

"I don't think it's because of greed. She must be in debt or something like that. You can never be sure, because even actresses and actors face financial problems," replied Nats.

"Hey Natasha and Kyle, I see you're back!" said Mom, interrupting our conversation.

"Oh, you woke up?" I asked, surprised by her sudden appearance.

"Yes, just a few seconds ago," replied Mom, her smile brightening the room.

"Hey Mrs. Peterson!" greeted Nats and Kyle in unison.

"You're just in time for dinner!" said Mom enthusiastically.

"We were worried that we might have missed it!" replied Kyle.

Mom stretched her hands out and yawned. "Mom, I'll make dinner, why don't you rest," I suggested.

"No thank you, Shelly, I can handle it! I am not sleepy anymore," declared Mom.

"Is that a tattoo, Mrs. Peterson?" asked Kyle, pointing to Mom's upper arm.

"I never noticed it either!" I remarked.

"Yes, it is!" said Mom cheerfully, proudly displaying the tattoo.

"GP, what does it stand for?" asked Nats.

"GP stands for Grace Peterson. I'm no longer Grace Malone," replied Mom. Her tone suggested she had found closure.

"Sorry about that," replied Kyle and Nats.

"It's alright, I'm over it now," said Mom.

"That's an amazing thing to do, Mom! You're a strong, independent woman!" I replied, and Mom came forward and gave me a hug.

"When did you get it, though?" I asked, curious about the timing of Mom's tattoo.

"Around 4 years ago, darling, right after my divorce," replied Mom.

"Nice!" remarked Nats.

"It's the best way to deal with it!" said Kyle.

"Yeah, it helped me a lot, trust me! I'll just have to do a few more things, and dinner shall be served!" declared Mom.

"Great! We can't wait!" I replied, and Mom smiled.

"By the way, I got an idea, we'll discuss it in T minus half an hour," I informed Kyle and Nats.

"A decoy, show us what you got!" remarked Kyle.

CHAPTER 23
The Decoy

"Dinner was delicious!" complimented Nats.

"That's flattering, thanks, dear," replied Mom with a smile.

"Now's the time," reminded Kyle, eager to get back to the matter at hand.

"Oh, yes! I totally forgot about it, thanks for the reminder," I said sarcastically.

"Kids, I'll sleep right now as I'm exhausted," informed Mom.

"Sure, Mom, I hope you don't mind us discussing the investigation," I said.

"No, not at all! But please don't shout," replied Mom.

"How about we go for a stroll and discuss it? That way, Mrs. Peterson won't be disturbed," suggested Kyle.

"Sounds good!" replied Nats.

"Okay, then, but come home before eleven," stated Mom.

"Sure, bye!" we said in unison as we left the house, eager to resume our discussion.

"Is your plan good?" asked Kyle excitedly.

"I don't know, but all I can say is that there's a fifty percent chance that it will work," I replied.

"Only fifty?" commented Nats.

"For now, yes, but after hearing your feedback, it might increase or decrease," I replied, acknowledging the uncertainty of our situation.

"Go on, we'll be silent," said Kyle.

"Did both of you receive Officer Jones' message?" I asked, wanting to ensure we were all on the same page.

"Yes, which means that Mr. Williams didn't survive," replied Nats, with regret but no surprise.

"They did their best to revive him, but unfortunately, they were unsuccessful in the end," I explained.

"So, what's the plan?" asked Kyle, changing the topic.

"Officer Jones and I had a discussion, and I suggested to him not to inform anyone about Mr. Williams' death after the attempt to revive him," I informed.

"Not even his family?" asked Kyle.

"Nope, not even Kayla. The reason being that only Kayla, Juliette, and maybe Jade know that he was in critical condition, but the others still believe he's alive. My plan won't work if Kayla, Juliette, and Jade know that he's been declared dead," I explained.

"I didn't understand a word of that!" exclaimed Kyle.

"Let me explain it to him in Kyle terms. See, while studying Mr. Williams' body, the doctors noticed his heartbeat was weakening. This evening, they tried to revive him. Only Kayla, Juliette, and maybe Jade knew about the revival attempt. But others like Shelly's mom, Trina, and Courtney don't know about this and think he is still alive. Now, Officer Jones confirmed that the doctors couldn't revive him, and they didn't inform Juliette and Kayla about this, so they still think he's being revived. Only a few of us, including you, me, Shelly, some cops, and the doctors, know the truth," clarified Nats.

"I got it! Shelly, you can continue," said Kyle, now fully understanding our plan.

"My plan is to publicly announce that Mr. Williams is conscious and will undergo interrogation before allowing any visitors. In the meantime, we'll replace Mr. Williams with a dummy on the hospital bed and wait for the perpetrator to make a move," I explained.

"What do you mean by 'wait for the perpetrator to come'?" asked Kyle.

"If the perpetrator learns that Mr. Williams is alive, she'll either flee New York immediately or attempt to kill him at the hospital to protect herself," I replied.

"Wouldn't it be easy for the perpetrator to escape?" questioned Nats.

"I've already thought of that! I've informed Officer Jones about my plan, and he's agreed to set up barricades beyond the jurisdiction of Green Avenue. Since the perpetrator is from Green Avenue, she won't be able to escape because the police will surround her. Her only option will be to attempt the kill," I explained.

"Suppose someone innocent enters Mr. Williams' room?" asked Kyle.

"We won't harm her or him, but we'll prevent anyone innocent from coming because Officer Jones will notify the residents of Green Avenue that the NYPD will deal with anyone attempting to visit the hospital," I answered.

"How will the criminal manage to break in if there's security?" asked Kyle.

"Excellent question! We'll intentionally keep security lax outside Mr. Williams' room or maybe even place just one guard there; otherwise, the killer will suspect it's a trap," I replied.

"So, there will be minimal security outside his room?" asked Nats.

"Only outside the room, not inside," I clarified.

"I didn't get you," replied Kyle.

"Other cops, including Officer Jones, will hide under the bed of Mr. Williams' dummy and will point their guns at the criminal if she tries to kill the dummy," I added.

"What if an innocent person comes to meet him?" asked Kyle.

"Is an innocent person capable of getting through the tight security at the entrance?" asked Nats.

"No, but there's loose security before his room," responded Kyle.

"A criminal can easily get through the tight security, and if it's too tight, we can try to make it moderate. I'm sure no one innocent would dare to move past the cops," replied Nats.

"She's right. Anyways, I wanted to discuss with you about our positions in the hospital," I said.

"We should be with the cops inside the room!" replied Nats cheerfully.

"No, hold on! We could get shot by her!" stated Kyle.

Yes, he's right. We can't act rashly. How about we pretend to be a cop and stand at the entrance?" I suggested.

"Why at the entrance when you can be inside the room and observe the criminal?" replied Nats.

"The entrance is the ideal spot because we can spot someone suspicious and inform the cops upstairs that security should be loose," I explained.

"That is wise, but I feel we should witness the live action. This is a once-in-a-lifetime opportunity to see a real-life criminal from a few feet away," replied Nats.

"If anyone must be in the room, it should be Shelly because she is composed and can remain silent until the criminal enters the room. If you're there, you'll make sounds, and the murderer can escape," explained Kyle.

"That sounds good because I just thought of a situation wherein the criminal approaches the room, sees no nurse, becomes suspicious, and decides not to enter. In that case, I'll stand right in front of the door. When the guilty enters, I'll calmly pretend to check on Mr. Williams and casually leave the room, waiting for her to make a move," I replied.

"But it's riskier than my idea, Shelly. You'll be right in front of the murderer! She can just point the gun at you, and within a second, you could meet Mr. Williams' fate," said Nats.

"Yes, it is risky. It may not work. What should we do then?" I asked.

"We could have one of the female cops dress up in a nurse's costume," suggested Nats.

"That makes sense because a cop can dodge bullets and fire them quickly as well," remarked Kyle.

"But I don't think the criminal will enter the room if there's a nurse," replied Kyle.

"No, she will enter the room and most likely shoot the nurse," I replied.

"Gosh! It's so confusing. What should we do?" asked Kyle.

"The nurse plan it is," I replied.

"What if the cop isn't able to respond quickly, and the killer shoots her instantly?" asked Kyle.

"The cop will be trained for such tasks," answered Nats.

"But the criminal will likely be more skilled at her task than the cop! We can't risk someone's life!" replied Kyle.

"The way he's describing the criminal's capabilities is starting to scare me," said Nats.

"Let's continue brainstorming more ideas," I stated.

Nats, Kyle, and I deliberated for a while but couldn't think of anything spectacular.

"Let's stick to the nurse idea then," I proposed..

"Don't worry about the nurse, Kyle. She can handle it," assured Nats.

Kyle nodded, but he didn't seem fully convinced by the idea.

"When exactly should we execute this?" asked Kyle.

"Tomorrow around half past nine, but not precisely at that time. We don't want to raise suspicions. The announcement about Mr. Williams' condition will be made shortly before nine, but not exactly at nine. Got it?" I clarified.

"Yes, and can I post the announcement on the Green Avenue forum?" asked Nats.

"I think it's best if the NYPD handles it," I replied.

"Too bad," remarked Nats.

"We should take a picture from a clever angle to depict Mr. Williams being interrogated, ensuring that it convinces the murderer that he's alive and well. We can stage the dummy holding a pen and appearing to write down answers!" suggested Nats.

"That's a good idea, but instead of having him hold a pen, we'll place a pen next to him and inform others that he's still feeble and trying his best to grasp the pen, but he can't. This approach is preferable because if the criminal observes him apparently writing answers, she will likely opt to flee instead of entering the room to harm him," explained Kyle.

"But we have that covered as well," replied Nats.

"But she can just make a U-turn and escape; if that happens, we would have failed to solve the crime, and eventually, the criminal would have realized that it was just a scam," I pointed out.

"Then what's the point of sealing the streets if she can just escape?" asked Kyle.

"To prevent them from leaving New York, but my main intention was to direct the criminal to the hospital rather than forcing them to escape. Sealing the streets was plan B, to be honest, and plan A was the hospital," I admitted.

"Shelly's right, we should not complicate things and let the pen be near the dummy but not in the dummy's hand," stated Nats, ending the discussion.

"I'll inform Officer Jones about our final plan," I said.

"Hope he agrees with us," said Kyle.

"We'll have to wait and see," replied Nats.

CHAPTER 24
Operation Gecko

"Wake up, Kyle!" Nats and I whispered, careful not to disturb Mom. "It's only six," Kyle grumbled sleepily. "We're late! We were supposed to be at the hospital by six!" replied Nats urgently. "Fine!" said Kyle as he quickly brushed his teeth and got dressed.

We hailed a cab and rushed to the hospital. Upon arrival, we hurried inside, knowing we were behind schedule.

"We've been waiting for you! You're half an hour late!" exclaimed Officer Jones.

"Sorry, Officer, I overslept," Kyle apologized.

"Do you guys have any last-minute questions about Operation Gecko?" Officer Jones inquired.

"Wait, what's Operation Gecko?" asked Kyle.

"Kyle, it's the name of our plan!" Nats clarified. "Oh, okay, I have no doubts whatsoever," Kyle replied. "Then let's get going," instructed Officer Jones as we headed upstairs to Mr. Williams' room.

"Nats, you handle Melissa's makeup, Kyle and I will take care of the dummy, the heart rate monitor, and the ventilator," I assigned tasks. We worked diligently and completed our assignments within an hour and a half. "Melissa, you look like a pretty good nurse!" praised Kyle.

"Thanks, and Natasha even designed a secret gun holder," replied Melissa.

"A white gun, nice!" I remarked.

"I painted it last night so that it goes with my skirt," she replied.

"Guys, Officer Jones posted the message!" announced Nats.

"Melissa, we'll have to go! All the best!" wished Kyle. "Thanks, and likewise!" replied Melissa as she closed the door.

"We got lame positions," said Nats. "The front is the most vital 'cause you can inform the cops about the criminal," I replied.

"I can guard the back entrance instead! I have a black belt in karate," Nats convinced.

"It's too late to change the plan," replied Kyle.

"But why does Shell get to be on the same floor close to Mr. Williams' room?" asked Nats.

"That's because Officer Jones wants me to notify him if the murderer makes it to this floor and attacks the cops," I explained.

"Fine, but next time, I'll be where there's action!" replied Nats.

"Go!" I urged, and Nats and Kyle left in a jiffy.

I positioned myself three feet away from Mr. Williams' room in a broom closet. I was extremely nervous because at the back of my head, the thought of the killer looking into the broom closet nagged me. There was a high possibility that she would try to hide in the broom closet and observe things from afar, but that was just a possibility. I clutched the walkie-talkie tightly and silently entered the closet and shut the door. I waited for an hour and didn't mind waiting longer as I wasn't claustrophobic. At last, I received a message from Nats, and she said, "The gecko has entered."

"Roger," I replied and remained vigilant. I looked through the small peephole inserted into the closet.

"The gecko has entered," came another voice from my walkie-talkie.

I was astonished as Nats had told me the same thing, but why did the cop repeat it?

I whispered, "Where was the gecko found?"

"At the back gate," he replied.

"But the gecko was found at the entrance as well," I replied, but I heard no reply.

According to what I just heard, there are two intruders! I knew it! The real murderer will never break into the hospital in the first place! I started to regret our plan and questioned what good I saw in it.

"Nats, Kyle, there are two intruders," I informed.

"What? Where's the second one?" asked Nats.

"At the back gate," I replied.

"Oh gosh! I'll inform the other cops," replied Nats.

I switched the channel of the walkie-talkie to Officer Jones and informed, "Officer, I'm afraid to say that there are two intruders."

"Really? I'm aware of the intruder at the entrance," he replied.

"There's another at the back gate. I got a message from another cop," I stated.

"Don't worry, I'll send Charlie. Just be vigilant because he or she will come to the second floor," replied Officer Jones.

"I'll be, and I'll ask you for reinforcement if we need any," I said.

"Great, GTG!" replied Officer Jones and ended the conversation.

I cautiously opened the door to check for any visible shadows. Just as I was about to open the door, a bullet whizzed past the closet and embedded into the wall. If I had opened the door five seconds ago, I would have been shot! I thanked my stars and promptly notified Officer Jones of the gunfire.

Through the peephole, I saw a cop rushing to the left with two of his companions. They pointed their guns to the wall opposite to the one the bullet embedded into and fired continuously, but one cop fell backward, shot from behind.

Sensing danger, I sent a distress signal to Officer Jones, knowing I could get caught if I made any noise. The firing continued for two minutes, which felt like an eternity. I curled myself up to evade any potential bullets.

After five agonizing minutes, the corridor fell silent, and my stomach churned with unease. I cautiously stood up and peered through the peephole. Both intruders lay on the floor alongside the fallen cop. The other two cops swiftly dragged them across the floor and rushed toward the exit.

I heard Officer Jones calling me, so I held the walkie-talkie to my ear.

"Abort mission!" he cried.

"Officer, why? The murderer isn't either of the two intruders. She's out there waiting for the right time to strike!" I replied.

"I lost one of my men, and I can't afford to lose more. Nine of my men are severely injured, and I can't risk your life as well! Come out of the closet! The cops are evacuating from Mr. Williams' room!" stated Officer Jones.

"Wait, Officer! We can't be hasty! Let's wait for half an hour. If there's no sign of the murderer, we'll evacuate," I convinced.

"Fine! I'm sending reinforcements just in case the murderer makes an appearance," he replied.

"Thank you, Officer, and I'm sorry that my plan backfired!" I spoke.

"Shit happens in life, and it's inevitable. You did a good job, kid," he assured and left the channel.

"Nats, things out here are crazy!" I informed.

"Yup, we were informed about it. I think she'll send more of her assistants to murder the dummy," replied Nats.

"Leave that place, Shelly! You could've gotten yourself killed!" insisted Kyle.

"Actually, I did! I was just about to open the closet's door when a bullet went straight past the door," I stated.

"Come then!" said Nats.

"I'll stay here for thirty minutes, and I'll be extra careful," I assured.

"Just be safe and contact us in case of an emergency," replied Nats worriedly.

"Don't worry, Nats! That's not like you," I replied.

"I know, but why are you acting brave like Natasha?" asked Kyle.

"I'm not! I just want to catch the criminal, and that's it!" I replied.

"Okay, chill! But promise that you won't get out of the closet!" demanded Nats.

"Fine, I won't! Bye!" I said and hung up.

I peered out of the peephole, searching for any signs of the murderer, but there was nothing. Ten minutes passed, and still, the floor remained deserted. "Shelly, I don't think she'll come," said Officer Jones.

"Officer, it's only been ten minutes. Let's wait for twenty more, please! I'm deeply sorry about the cop who lost his life, but I'm confident the criminal will surface today," I pleaded.

"Twenty minutes, and that's final," replied Officer Jones.

Frustration boiled inside me, and I pounded the closet door loudly. I had been so close to apprehending the criminal! Sitting down, I began counting to two thousand. After twenty-five agonizing minutes, I conceded defeat and contemplated calling off the operation when a voice crackled through my walkie-talkie.

"Apologies, could you repeat your message?" I responded.

"Olivia has been killed! She was on the hospital terrace, her walkie-talkie missing, and she's dressed in someone else's clothes!" informed a male cop.

"Damn it! Olivia was crucial to the operation! I'm dispatching reinforcements to the first floor," replied Officer Jones.

"Understood, Officer!" I acknowledged before ending the call.

Becoming increasingly vigilant, I glanced out of the peephole again and spotted a female cop wearing sunglasses. She approached the broom closet, and I held my breath, hoping to evade detection. My heart raced as she pressed her ear against the closet, listening intently. After a tense minute, she decided to move on. Exhaling deeply, I sent an emergency signal to Officer Jones and all the cops. They reacted swiftly, informing me, "Shelly, the entrance to the first floor is sealed from both sides!"

"What? Should we try shooting bullets?" I suggested.

"But that could allow the criminal to escape," replied Officer Jones.

"Are you certain it's her?" inquired a cop.

"Absolutely," I affirmed without hesitation.

"Where is she now?" asked Officer Jones.

"I don't know! I'll have to leave the closet to find out. Should I?" I inquired.

"No, it's too risky for you," insisted Officer Jones.

"But you taught her how to use a gun," pointed out another cop.

"Even so, no!" Officer Jones reiterated firmly.

"We're in a dilemma, what should we do?" I pondered aloud when, the next moment, a knock sounded at a nearby door.

"She knocked on Mr. Williams' room," I informed.

"We have to act now!" ordered Officer Jones.

The gunfire erupted, and the door was unlocked. To our astonishment, the murderer had reinforcements, and returned fire. Terrified, I curled up, waiting for the chaos to subside. After what felt like an eternity, the gunfire ceased, and I cautiously opened the door, rushing toward the commotion.

Entering the room, I found it enveloped in a purple gas, likely from a smoke bomb. "Stay back, nurse, unless you want to die," the murderer threatened.

"I won't yield," retorted Melissa defiantly.

"Then I have no choice," replied the murderer, firing a shot.

"Oh no! You've killed Henry!" Melissa cried out in a feigned tone.

"I have no business with you now," declared the murderer,

shooting at the window to escape.

Acting quickly, I lunged toward her, ripping off her glasses. To my surprise, she didn't turn back, fleeing toward the window. In pursuit, I grasped at her dress. As Melissa raised her gun, poised to fire, I shouted, "Look behind you, there's no escaping now, Mom!"

CHAPTER 25
The Truth

Mom turned back instantly, her expression one of disbelief. "Yeah, I knew about it for a long time now!" I vented out. Instead of replying, she brought out another smoke bomb and hurled it near me.

"She's your mom?" asked Melissa. I couldn't find words to respond, grappling with the shock myself.

"Catch her!" ordered Melissa. The cops hiding under the bed emerged, but Mom's accomplices obstructed them.

"Don't even take a step, Shelly!" one of them threatened me. "Just because you're Grace's daughter doesn't mean we'll make an exception for you," cried another.

"Oh, you will," replied a cop, swiftly shooting the two assailants. Melissa and the cops dashed toward the entrance to prevent Mom from escaping.

"Shelly, don't follow us!" instructed Melissa.

"I want to!" I insisted, disregarding her caution.

"Roger, guard Shelly," instructed Melissa.

"Yes Ma'am! Shelly, follow me," said Roger.

"She's attempting to leave the hospital," I promptly informed Officer Jones.

"We are at the entrance gate," replied Officer Jones.

Melissa and the cops reached the gate before us, and I was panting for breath.

"Are you okay, Shelly?" asked Roger.

"Yes, I'm fine. Let's go!" I said, and we finally reached the gate. Mom was surrounded by the NYPD. After being apprehended by me, Mom donned a mask to conceal her identity.

"Give up and surrender yourself to the NYPD!" ordered Officer Jones.

Mom didn't budge and sprinted as fast as she could, but Melissa caught her and cuffed Mom to herself.

"Who are you?" asked Mr. Gary, approaching Mom and removing her mask. I was stunned to see Mr. Gary involved in the operation.

"Grace!" exclaimed Officer Jones. Nats and Kyle were shaken and struggled to comprehend what was unfolding.

"This has to be a mistake!" cried Nats.

"It can't be Mrs. Peterson! Shelly, back us up!" pleaded Kyle.

I remained silent, feeling helpless. "Shelly, why aren't you saying anything?" asked Nats.

"It isn't a mistake," I mumbled softly, noticing Mom's sneaky glance at me.

"Mrs. Peterson, this is a mistake, right?" asked Kyle.

Mom felt a pang of humiliation and didn't respond.

"The dreadful thought of Mom being the culprit crossed my mind yesterday, but I dismissed it as irrational. However, by nightfall, it started to make more sense. I held onto a sliver of hope that I was overthinking, but Mom proved me right!

"Was it necessary to kill Henry? That guy was a jerk, but you could've revealed the truth instead of taking revenge!" I broke down.

"No one would've believed me as I didn't have proof! Pierce was killed by Henry, but no one believed Aidyl! The doctor declared that he was poisoned, but there was no evidence that it was Henry! We requested an investigation, but they declined our offers, which was absurd. That was when I realized that it was Henry's elaborate plan to win the **** case!" swore Mom.

"You never even told me about Pierce! You cheated on Dad with him, didn't you?" I asked.

"No, after our divorce, I dated him," replied Mom. Nats and Kyle were in a trance, clueless about what was going on.

"We'll have to take away Grace," informed Officer Jones.

"I have no one now! Dad doesn't care about me, and you've made the biggest mistake of your life! I have no family and am all alone! I was alone to begin with and in the end as well! I'll never forgive you!" I cried bitterly.

"Instead of forgiving me, can you please clear the allegations on Pierce? I can never expect you to forgive me after what I did, but I'm truly sorry," apologized Mom.

I didn't respond and turned to go to Nats and Kyle's side. Mom hugged me from behind, and I stopped instantly, turning to face her, giving her one last hug.

"Please visit me whenever you can. Thank you for everything, Shelly," said Mom, wiping a tear from her cheek. I couldn't hold back my tears any longer, and neither could she. Mom and I would have to walk different paths now; that was our fate. She went to the left, and I went to the right, teary-eyed, helpless, and confused. That's how we parted.

CHAPTER 26
The bitter-sweet ending

"Shelly, you were wrong about one thing," said Kyle.

"What?" I asked dully.

"You aren't alone! Nats and I are with you; we are your family," he replied, and both hugged me.

"Thank you for everything, but I don't know what to do," I replied.

"You can't give up! You have a job," reminded Nats.

"I had one, but I got fired, remember?" I replied.

"You have a new one at the LAPD!" announced Officer Jones excitedly.

"What? Did you do this, Officer Jones?" I asked.

"I have a friend in LA, and I gave you a letter of recommendation, and he instantly decided to hire you. Congratulations!" explained Officer Jones.

"Thank you so much!" I replied and hugged him.

"You deserved it, kiddo. If it wasn't for the three of you, we couldn't have cracked the case," appreciated Officer Jones.

"Can you give us letters of recommendation as well?" asked Kyle.

"I can, actually," replied Officer Jones.

"I was just kidding," said Kyle, and Nats and Officer Jones laughed nervously.

"Actually, it was Natasha's idea to give you a letter of recommendation," stated Officer Jones.

"Really, thanks, Nats!" I replied.

"No problem, you have a more thrilling job now," she said.

"Can you tell us how exactly you realized that Grace was the murderer?" asked Officer Jones.

"I guess that was the most awaited question, so I'll answer it for you. I went to the bathroom in the south wing yesterday where I found a secret passage to Mr. Williams' room. I went through it and reached his room through a hole in the wall covered by a plank. That's when I realized that the murderer was the person in the bathroom. I saw the video of the Mystery Lady once again and noticed that she seemed to have emerged from the bathroom after attacking Mr. Williams. I recalled that Mom was in the bathroom in the north wing, directly opposite to the south wing's, and the thought of Mom being in the south wing bathroom dawned on me. I tried to retrace my steps on the day of the party and realized that Nats insisted that Mom went south, but Kyle said that Mom went north. Aidyl also said that Mom went south and when we went there, no one responded, but the door was locked. What if Mom was actually in that bathroom, and someone covered for her in the north wing bathroom?" I explained.

"We heard her voice, Shelly," replied Kyle.

"It was a recording that Aidyl played, and this is where Aidyl comes into the picture. After talking with us, Aidyl disappeared and only came during the end of the masquerade ball. She was in the north bathroom the entire time and played recordings of Mom's voice. Mom must have prepared many messages for various situations, and she created enough scenarios for everything to go smoothly. I distinctly remember Mom repeating the same sentence three times, each with identical voice modulation and duration. While it initially seemed normal, upon reflection, I grew suspicious. To be completely sure, I checked Mom's voice clips but couldn't find any."

"Mystery Lady's belongings were intentionally placed in everyone's flats except Jade's to make her look suspicious," I added.

"But why did she let herself get caught temporarily?" asked Kyle.

"To avoid suspicion. All the members of the Welfare Committee owned the Mystery Lady's belongings except for Jade, which was fishy. Jade had access to Trina, Mom, and Courtney's flats so she could have placed them easily. Because of that incident, we interrogated Jade, and Mom thought that it would buy her time to escape, but thanks to Jade, we learned about Pierce Ackleman. I purposely mentioned Pierce's name to Mom, and she was shocked, which further solidified my suspicions. The final clue that led me to think that Mom did it was when I saw her tattoo," I continued.

"What's wrong with that?" Nats asked, puzzled by the significance of the initials "GP" written within a heart.

"GP stood for Grace and Pierce. Mom dated Pierce Ackleman and only pretended to love Henry to get close to him and eventually kill him. After Pierce's death, Mom was devastated and plotted her revenge. She must have taken martial arts classes and would have learned how to kill Mr. Williams with any sharp object," I stated.

"That seems farfetched. Do you know which weapon she used?" asked Officer Jones.

"She used her fake hairclip, which was actually a martial arts weapon. I'm not sure which martial art it's from, but it's definitely that. If you watch the video again, you can see that the Mystery Lady has a long clip on the side of her head. Also, Wayne said that he heard a thud while leaving the room before seven, and that was when Mom jumped out of the hole in the wall. As for the burning smell that Ms. Clover smelled, Mom burned his letter to destroy evidence but didn't have time to dispose of it properly, so she left it amongst Mr. Williams' clothes.

"How exactly was Rosa involved in this plan?" questioned Nats.

"I'm not entirely sure, but I'm guessing that she helped Aidyl get to the north bathroom by allowing her to hide underneath the trolley that waitresses use to serve food. I might be imagining things, but I think that was her role," I replied.

"That sounds plausible to me. But why didn't you tell us about these things?" asked Nats.

"I only confided in Officer Jones about suspecting Mom because I thought I was being irrational, and these thoughts only occurred to me after I visited the bathroom in the south wing," I replied.

"You are a genius, Shelly!" exclaimed Kyle.

"Thanks, but I think that's an overstatement," I said.

"I can't believe there's a secret passage in Henry's house. The NYPD will ensure it's sealed to prevent further incidents,," said Officer Jones.

"Where are we going now?" I asked.

"To the Mayor's house for one last visit," replied Officer Jones, escorting us into his van. We arrived within ten minutes and headed to the bathroom. After sealing the passage, we went upstairs and had snacks.

"Sir, you have a visitor," said Wayne.

"Who is it?" asked Officer Jones.

"I thought we weren't allowed to let anyone in," replied Wayne.

"We can now, but who is it?" questioned Officer Jones.

"It's Ms. Kayla, and she has come to thank the NYPD and the detectives," informed Wayne.

"Let her in," said Officer Jones.

"I can't believe she wants to thank us," I commented.

"Well, she should, considering how much we helped her out," replied Kyle.

"Well said, Kyle! I'm glad you're over that *****" praised Nats.

"Also, Nats, will you go out with me someday?" asked Kyle, suddenly.

"How about now?" said Nats and grabbed his hand as they headed downstairs, leaving me behind.

"This will be interesting," I said as I followed them. My mind was consumed by thoughts of Mom.

I hoped I could forgive her someday...